INSPECTOR MAGE

BLOOD ON THE FLOOR

ALEESE HUGHES

Writ Keepers Publishing

BOOK ONE OF *THE INSPECTOR MAGE TRILOGY*

Published by Writ Keepers Publishing

ISBN: 9798587727342

❀ Created with Vellum

~

For my sister Ilana—the one who loves books just as much as I do. Keep writing, sis!

CONTENTS

MAP

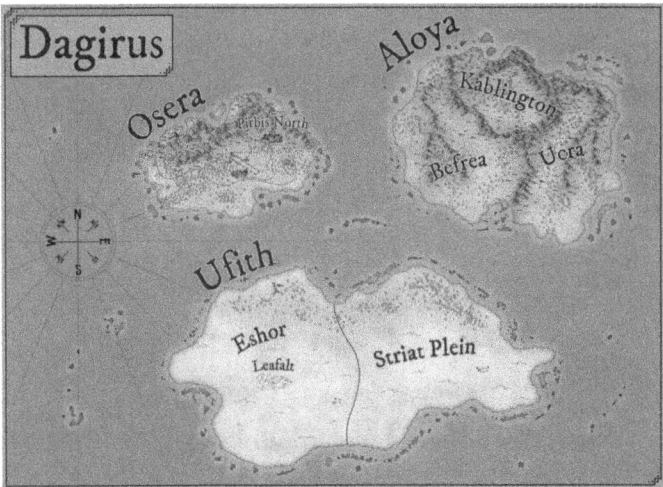

The World of Dagirus

1

Russell

INSPECTOR RUSSELL GAINES RIPPED ONE OF MANY clipped news articles from the bulletin board. Now three years old, it read:

"New Age God Kills Heir to Hill Family Fortune."

Russell snagged a second clipping from the past year:

"Woman Dies by Asphyxiation; New Age God Suspected."

The final article Russell procured from the bulletin board told of a more recent death: a nine-year-old boy. Battered and bloodied, he had been found in the street with a note hammered into his collarbone with a long, silver nail. The boy was among a dozen victims, victims the police *knew* of, killed by the New Age God.

Russell bent his head to study the papers in his hands. His golden-brown hair fell in front of his eyes as he did so. It had been much too long since he'd seen a barber.

The Pirbis North Daily had written about the New Age God for three years now. Every time an edition came out with the wretched man's self-proclaimed name in its headline, Russell's stomach tied itself into painful knots.

The killer's motives lacked clarity—not enough for Russell, or anyone else, to determine his next moves. Initially, the killer targeted rich, middle-aged men. That was followed by male *and* female victims—both poor and wealthy. The pattern's most puzzling and disturbing changes arose in the past year as the New Age God began killing children and dumping their bodies out on the street.

"They're all Oseran, though," Russell muttered to himself, returning his gaze to the bulletin board. "That means they all had Mage Gifts."

Russell studied the pictures at the top of each clipping: gruesome, black-and-white images of the victims. Some were stabbed, some beaten, some suffocated. Their deaths were all so random.

Was that intentional?

Russell repinned the news articles to their designated spots on the board. He reached into one of his many coat pockets, and with a quick intake of breath, withdrew a piece of paper.

It was the very note nailed so brutally to that little boy's collar bone. Russell had grabbed it before the other policemen could place it into evidence. He took it because it seemed to be addressing him. It didn't say as much, but Russell knew the New Age God well enough to read between the lines. Besides, it wasn't the first letter the New Age God had directed to Russell—all threatening, some mocking, and many displaying the killer's enjoyment of this game he was playing with Russell.

But there was one major difference between this letter and the others: It wasn't coded. The New Age God took pleasure in leaving cryptic messages to Russell. Each was written in code, and the code changed with every note, forcing Russell to decipher each one—a process the world mistakenly assumed came naturally to him.

But this note, the one Russell clutched in his hands and gazed at now, could be read by anyone:

THIS IS TOO EASY. YOU NEED TO MOVE FASTER IF YOU DON'T WANT ANY BLOOD ON YOUR HANDS.

Russell read the note aloud. He had pored over those neatly written words *at least* a couple hundred times, and they still offered no more clues than his first time reading them.

Russell Gaines held quite a reputation in Pirbis North—a reputation as the best inspector in the city, maybe even in all of Osera. Russell was in his early twenties and had served only a short time as a police officer, which would typically keep him away from dangerous and complex cases. Yet, he had led the investigation of the notorious serial killer almost from the beginning. Chief Augustus Marsh, head of the city's police department, believed Russell was the only one capable of taking on such a daunting job. And even the New Age God, like everyone else, wouldn't dare underestimate Russell Gaines. The letter was for Russell—he just knew it.

Next to the final word on the note was an image of a crescent moon made by a black stamp. It was a symbol the New Age God had purloined from the Oseran God Othos. Upon closer inspection many weeks ago, Russell could tell the killer had pressed the heavily inked stamp into the paper so hard that he had ripped a small section of the note at the tip of the crescent moon.

Russell groaned in frustration and clutched the note in his grip with a tight fist that bore his cracked, dry skin—a souvenir from a freezing winter spent trudging throughout the city. The inspector ground his teeth and paced the length of the room.

"He wants to feel powerful," Russell breathed, tapping his fingers against his thighs as he walked. "He likes having control."

The door to the empty room, save for the long bulletin board at its center, opened with a soft *whoosh*; the cold air from the hall outside made Russell shiver.

"Gaines?" Chief Marsh came in through the door. "You're still here?"

The first year of marriage was beginning to show on the chief. Marsh once prided himself on his fit and slender build, but now more than a few pounds padded his belly, stretching his police uniform. Just another reason Russell tacked onto his growing mental list to avoid marriage, or any romantic attachment, at all costs.

Marsh blew out a long breath of air, pushing his lips out along with his neat, curly mustache. "I thought you left *hours* ago."

He clasped his hands behind his back and approached the bulletin board with a slow, disbelieving shake of the head.

Russell continued to pace. "I feel so close!" he stormed, pounding his fists against his legs. "But he keeps eluding me."

Marsh tilted his head, and his soft blue eyes met Russell's with such intensity it made Russell shrink back.

"Go home, Gaines. You're no good to us without rest. Look..." He pointed at Russell's hazel eyes as the inspector realized they were drooping. "I don't think your Gift will work well without any sleep, either."

Russell placed two fingers under each of his eyes. Marsh was right—it *was* challenging to think, let alone use his Mage Gift for Marsh's benefit without having slept. Wait, when *had* he last slept?

"Go home. Everything will be here when you get back."

"But—"

Marsh held up a hand. "*Go.*"

∿

RUSSELL STOOD at the bottom of the broad stone steps leading away from the police building. He hugged his coat tight as the chill wind nipped at him. Russell didn't want to call George at such a late hour to pick him up, and walking home didn't appeal to him either. Sighing, Russell peered through the dark streets in the hopes he could find a mage carriage for hire.

With invention and industrialization still relatively new in Osera, buggies pulled by horses were still more common than the newer mage carriages. But Russell predicted that would change in another three years or so.

"Oh, please be a cab," Russell said aloud as the lights of a small vehicle made their way in his line of vision. He flung a hand up into the air and waved and whistled at the mage carriage as it cruised along the city street.

The tiny, black carriage pulled up. The man sitting at the steering wheel was clad in dark clothing, his face covered by a kerchief, and his stout body wrapped in a multitude of scarves atop a thick coat, all to protect himself against the brutal cold of Pirbis North. His gloved hands remained firmly planted on the tall wheel in front of him.

"Uh, hello," Russell said, approaching the opened window and proffering a smile. The mysterious man did not offer even a glance in the inspector's direction. Or, at least, Russell *thought* he didn't. He could barely see the tops of the man's eyes beneath all the clothing obscuring his features.

"Are you a cab? I need to get to Senna Lane. You know it?"

The kerchief around the driver's face bobbed up and down as the man gave a quick nod.

"Great!" Russell clapped his hands together. The sound echoed along the empty streets.

Still smiling, Russell made his way to the back of the carriage. He fumbled a bit with the metal handle of the vehicle's back door before clambering inside.

Russell shivered as he sat on the cold leather seat. His breath continued to create clouds in front of his face as the mage carriage provided no heat. But it wouldn't surprise him if that problem was solved by the Meltons, a family of inventors, within the next few years.

"I don't like the winter." Russell sniffled as his nose began to run from the biting, chill air, then nearly gagged as the strong smell of sardines overwhelmed him. What had the driver done—spill an entire can over the seats?

But even with his dislike of the cold, Russell had to admit the piles of snow sparkling on the peaks of the mountaintops surrounding the city was breathtaking.

"The cold weather is horrid, but the mountains look really nice this time of year," Russell said, trying to spark some small talk.

The driver still made no sound as he slammed a foot down on the pedal, activating the force gems within the vehicle's hood, and drove the carriage forward.

Russell's muscles tightened at the roaring sound of the larger force gems flaring up to increase speed.

His pulse quickened. "Uh, you're going kind of fast, don't you think?"

The man only sped up. The vehicle screeched as its wheels made sharp turns down the narrow city roads. Russell pressed himself against the back of his tall seat, fearful the driver would lose control of the vehicle and hit one of the many streetlamps lining their path. The carriage tumbled down the road so quickly that the city's tall buildings and the bright lights used by late-night party-goers whizzed by in a blur.

"Will you slow down, please?"

Again, no answer. Russell clenched his fists and dared himself to lean forward just until his mouth was close to the driver's ear.

"You're going to kill us! Slow down *now*," Russell demanded.

The mysterious man didn't so much as flinch at his words. Russell pinched his lips together, then sat back to see how close they were to home while thinking of ways he could escape the vehicle without too much injury. Soon, they made it to the block that held the Gaines' family mansion.

"My house is right—" Russell stopped, realizing the man was already beginning to speed his way in to park in front of the mansion.

"Wait," he said aloud, realization striking him

like a punch in the face, "I only gave you the street name. How do you know my house? Have we met?"

Russell's stomach lurched, both from the terrible feeling rising inside of him and the way the carriage was ping-ponging off the curb as it pulled in. Just as the carriage came to a screeching stop, Russell pressed his weight on the door and tumbled out. He wasn't going to spend any more time than necessary in an enclosed space with this lunatic.

Russell released a small sigh of relief at the sight of his five-story home, with its familiar stone walls and neat lawns. He turned to the driver.

"You really should *not* work for the cab service if you drive like that."

Russell straightened the fedora atop his head and took a few steps away from the mage carriage, making sure he was at least a few arms' lengths away. He made no move to retrieve payment—not after *that* ride.

Without a look in the inspector's direction, the darkly clad man slipped a hand from the steering wheel and into his coat pocket. Within a fraction of a second, the hand returned with a tightly folded sheet of yellow paper gripped between two fingers.

Russell narrowed his eyes. "For me?"

With a single, curt nod, and the quick flick of his fingers, the note flew out of the driver's side window and onto the cobblestones at Russell's feet. He jumped back as if the paper would explode.

"What is this? Is it from you?" Russell looked up at the mysterious man, but he was already slamming a foot on the pedal to speed away.

The inspector scratched at the stubble on his cheek and approached the paper on the ground. Something bulged at its center, weighing the paper down enough to keep it from blowing away in the wind.

"What in Othos' name?" he whispered, scooping the object into his hand.

He drew in a sharp breath at the sight of an inked symbol that partially appeared from underneath a fold.

"No, it can't be," he whispered.

He hurriedly opened the yellow paper and saw a hint of a sparkle as the moonlight danced on its contents.

It was a hairpin—a beautiful pin decorated with a neat line of pearls. Russell recognized it as his sister's. Sweet little ten-year-old Amelia wore that pin everywhere—even to bed.

But how...?

Bile formed in Russell's mouth as he looked at the paper's words, uncoded, same as the previous letter:

I'M SURPRISED THE GREAT INSPECTOR GAINES NEEDED ANOTHER HINT. I HOPE YOU WERE ABLE TO SAY YOUR GOODBYES.

And right at the end of the daunting words was what he feared he had seen just as he'd picked up the paper: a dark, crescent moon, stamped in black ink.

2

Five years later...

Julie

I walked along the narrow halls of my home, long fingers running against the walls' smooth, baby blue paper. Things were chaotic at the manor as preparations were made for my engagement party. I passed the entire staff of fifty servants as they shouted out directions, hung colored ribbons, and ran to and from the grand ballroom with silver platters of steaming food.

I stopped in a dark corner to observe one maid, Laura Smith. The short woman flicked a finger and levitated a single piece of shining gold ribbon along the banister of the marble staircase. Her Mage Gift allowed her to levitate any inanimate object. It had always been a great help to Laura in performing her duties at the manor.

I sighed inwardly, careful not to make too much noise as I moved toward another hallway. I didn't feel like conversing with anyone just an hour before I had to spend an immense amount of energy entertaining the guests and my fiancé.

"Hi, Miss Julie!"

I winced at the sound of Laura's piercing voice. Of course my bad luck would summon just the thing I didn't want to deal with.

My shoulders curled forward, which caved my chest in as I reluctantly turned to Laura and summoned a weak smile.

"Hello, Laura."

The woman beamed at me and bounced on the balls of her feet as she approached. Though Laura was well into her thirties, she had the exuberance of a child. Not that I judged her for it. My twenties had not yet taken away my enthusiasm—at least for some things.

"We have a new maid who just started today!"

My strained smile faltered even more as I feared her next words. "Oh?"

"She is thrilled to work for your family, and she *especially* admires yours and Lord Melton's Gifts!"

My mouth went dry. The Melton family, my family, held a certain fame for our Mage Gifts. Every Oseran was born with one. Our religion taught that Othos, God of Beginnings, and the most *powerful* mage in existence, created Dagirus five millennia ago and placed upon it three large continents: Osera, Aloya, and Ufith. But Othos favored Osera and bestowed upon its people Mage Gifts. These Gifts gave their recipients different abilities. Some could summon fire from their hands, others could levitate things, and a few could even fly.

The more powerful your Gift, the higher class your family. And some individuals, even if born into a lower-class family, were born with more powerful and useful Gifts. They had a chance for social elevation by marrying well and sharing their Gifts with future children.

Fifty lording families presided over the districts in Osera, including my own. For centuries, each family bred with other lords and ladies to maintain their bloodline and powerful Mage Gifts. But even Oserans outside of the lording families had a Gift. Every Oseran except me.

"The new maid—Alice is her name—she was hoping to catch you and ask if you could show her an illusion."

I could barely hear Laura over my thoughts. But even as she said it, I instinctively reached for the necklace tied around my neck—one of the objects that had aided in my farce for so many years. I had only one with me—an unusual occurrence. I would typically have at *least* three necklaces hidden in the pockets I'd personally sewn into all of my clothing, but the party dress I wore had no such hidden compartments. I hated wearing dresses.

My hand tightened over the small locket at the end of the necklace's chain, and I gulped. I'd used this particular necklace on more than one occasion, and Laura's query reminded me to ask Father and Mother to create a new illusion necklace for the party.

"Is she here?" I croaked, darting my eyes about in search of the maid in question.

"No, she had to help in the kitchens, but she hoped I could ask for you to display your Gift at the party tonight." Laura suddenly flushed and stared at her shuffling feet. "That is, if you wish to, Miss Melton."

I dropped the necklace back into its resting position above my collar bone, relief flooding over me. I didn't have to create an illusion immediately. I had time.

"Of course." My eyes crinkled up with a large

smile. "Tell her I'll have something special prepared."

Laura giggled, flipped her strawberry-blond hair away from her face, thanked me profusely, then scurried away and back to her work.

I let out a long breath of air and turned quickly away, heading back in my intended direction. After a few steps, my muscles relaxed. Even without the decoration for the party, my family's manor always had a certain...elaborate beauty. A soft couch rested in every corridor, about a dozen paintings of different flowers and scenery hung on every wall, and sparkling light gems dangled from nearly every inch of the ceiling. Mother was not one for a minimalist lifestyle. She liked things, and she enjoyed making her home as pretty and welcoming as possible.

I halted in the middle of the hall and sighed, looking longingly at one of the many sofas beckoning me to recline on its yellow cushions and take a nap. Of course, there was no time, but shutting my eyes and escaping my responsibilities appealed to me.

Shaking my head, I continued my walk. The loose dress I was wearing swayed uncomfortably at my knees, allowing the chill air to move up the short gown and tickle my unprotected skin. I would much prefer my regular trousers to this party dress.

Scratch that; I would even prefer the long gowns that had been in style nearly a decade ago. They were definitely warmer.

Why the short, straight dresses? I thought. I stopped walking and shook the frills hanging from the shimmering, pinkish-tan dress's hemline.

They don't even flatter a woman's figure. Well, they don't flatter mine *anyway.*

Not that I cared for showing off my curves. I had them, sure, but I was so tall no man ever paid attention to the decent parts of me. Mother always said my height gave me an elegant beauty. And, of course, that was her way of making her child feel better.

I shivered, hugging myself against the cold.

Why didn't Mother replace the broken heat gem? All we have are the fire gems in our hearths. And it wasn't like Mother couldn't easily supply a working heat gem, what with her Mage Gift and all.

I squeezed my eyes shut, forcing my thoughts away from Mother's Gift. It was not a good day to pine over and wish to have inherited her incredible ability.

I turned another corner and smiled as I saw my mother staring at her reflection in a wall mirror and poking at her hair. Mother's golden locks were pinned immaculately in large curls on her head, making the hair that reached past her shoulders seem only chin length. I placed a hand on my own dark hair. Mother had sent a hairdresser into my room earlier that day to apply a similar style to my own locks.

"Julie! There you are!" She beamed at me warmly. Mother was already in her evening gown. It was slightly longer than mine and colored a deep blue with various sequins and sparkles. She held out her arms, gesturing for me to come into her embrace.

I smiled. Mother's presence alone eased the chill in my body. One could never resist feeling warm and optimistic when she was nearby.

I melted into Mother's arms, reminded of my childhood days when her embrace had been all I craved. She smelled like fresh-baked cookies and flowery perfume. And even now, though I had grown taller than my sister and even my father, Mother towered over me like a well-mannered, comforting storm.

Mother pulled away; her gray eyes scanned me up and down.

"You look so nice, dear," she gushed.

I snorted. "I despise dressing up. You know that."

Mother wrinkled her nose in amusement and fondly brushed a stray strand of my chestnut hair behind my ear.

"But plodding about at your engagement party in men's clothing will not do. *You* know that."

I rolled my eyes but continued to smile. Of course, she was right, and I was willing to make a good impression on the guests and my betrothed. Even so, I would never enjoy fashion and looking pretty as much as my mother did.

Mother took one of my hands in her own. Although she was well into middle-age, the ivory skin on her hands and face remained young and almost entirely free of lines, save for the little crinkles at the edges of her eyes.

"Come, love," she whispered with a twinkle in her eye, "I want to show you our latest invention."

I grinned. "Yes, please!"

Mother extended her elbow, and I eagerly looped my arm into hers as we walked.

"You remind me so much of your grandmother."

My heart radiated through my fingertips. Mary Lindon, my maternal grandmother, had been an amazing woman. Brilliant, beautiful, and, of course, she had a powerful Mage Gift. A Gift that Mother and my sister, Eliza, inherited. It was the greatest Gift in modern history: They could copy *any* other person's Gift and place it into a gem.

How it worked was simplicity personified. My mother, or anyone else with a Gift like hers, would just have to grasp a gem, touch the person carrying the Gift she wished to copy, then will that person's ability *into* the gem. No harm came to either involved. However, limits existed. Once an object had a Gift within it, no other abilities could be placed there.

After years of experimentation, Grandmother learned certain gems had varying levels of the copied Gifts' potencies. An opal stone, for instance, would provide a highly diluted copy of the Gift. But a diamond, specifically a blue diamond, would have astounding levels of Gift use.

I couldn't begin to count how many times I wished to have inherited Grandmother's Gift just as Mother and my sister had, so Mother's compliment warmed me more than I could say.

"Really?" I whispered.

Mother nodded. "Really. Your excitement for new advancements lights up your entire face and sets a kind of fiery passion in your eyes."

I released a deep, gratifying sigh. What she said rang true. I adored watching Mother use her ability to work with others' Gifts and create new devices that aided in advancing the modern world.

"When your grandmother first invented the mage carriage," Mother continued, "she wanted more than anything to share it with the world so others might enjoy the benefits of a machine that could take a person from place to place in a *fraction* of the time a horse could."

Mother's soft expression made my smile grow.

"You are like that, Julie. You enjoy helping and contributing to the world in whatever ways you can."

I drew my lips into a thin line. What could she mean? I had no Gift. I didn't invent things, and I couldn't help out *anyone* due to my deficiencies.

"Here we are."

Mother retracted herself from my side and pushed open the bright yellow door leading to her study.

"It's on my desk," she said.

I clutched my hands together, suddenly forgetting my self-loathing. Mother's office was cluttered. Blueprints and sketch pads lay strewn all over her desk and the burgundy carpet, but it was somehow comforting. To me, it almost represented the noble work my brilliant mother accomplished every day.

I scurried my way over to the desk once I saw it. Eyes wide, I lifted the iron model consisting of a thin tube with wings attached to its sides.

"What is it?" I breathed.

"It's a flying mage carriage!" she exclaimed, approaching from behind and gently taking the model into her grip. She held the cumbersome object in both hands and moved it up and through the air above her head as if demonstrating what it was supposed to do. "At least, that's the idea."

I cocked my head. "Wait, you mean like the mage carriages we drive through the streets, but this one will fly?" I clapped my hands together. "How big? How fast? When?"

Mother clicked her tongue, chiding me as she placed the model back onto her long desk.

"You know better, Julie. These things take time. Scientists say we'll need steel, of which Aloya has an abundance. But the force gem we need has to be quite large, and the actual machine will take a good deal of metal." She tapped a long fingernail against her chin.

"We'll need a few force gems, actually. It'll work much like a mage carriage, where it uses gems to create motion and speed, but it will take a lot more power. And some gravity-resistance gems."

I pursed my lips, thinking about what she'd said. It made sense, if the machine was to be as big as she suggested.

"Where will all the material come from? I assume you want to make more than one. I thought the Supreme Minister had significantly raised tariffs for foreign trading. Aloya can afford to export to us?"

Mother shook her head. "They're actually only increased for Ufith. Supreme Minister said it was one of the initiatives to start collecting debts from the harm and destruction Ufith brought about in the war."

Mother bowed her head and glued her stormy eyes to the carpet at our feet. She never liked discussing politics. After the four-year war that an Ufith king had started against the entirety of Dagirus ended, which happened only a few months ago, those in power making benefits and convenience available only to the higher class became even more of an issue than before. And those outside of such families and powerful positions were charged higher taxes and forced to work the farms and gem mines.

I didn't follow it too closely, but such laws against the poor had a lot to do with Osera's growing dislike of immigrants from enemy countries. Mixing the blood of immigrants and Oserans was highly frowned upon, and the result created more separation among the different people. Half-Oserans were just as ostracized as non-Oserans.

I chose not to push the subject and instead wandered around the cozy room. A long wooden table displayed not only Mother's achievements and inventions but also Grandmother's.

The table began with Grandmother Mary's first invention: the fire gem. I touched the ruby. It was much too large and heavy to hold and was cold and inactive at the moment.

The story behind its creation was a family legend. Forty years ago, Grandmother had approached a lord from the west side of Osera. He had the strongest fire-related Mage Gift in the country. He could catch anything, or anyone, on fire with just a thought. After a few weeks of collaboration, they created the perfect object to rest in the hearths that once held logs and coal. Grandmother used her Gift to copy the lord's and place it into a ruby—a gem strong enough to maintain a long-lasting burn from a fire Gift.

The invention changed the world forever. Grandmother always said she had never been more tired than when she first created the fire gem. The demand for it was intense, but a lack of supply in rubies, a rare and precious stone, made supply hard to come by. Taxes were increased on the invention, and soon only the rich could get their hands on them.

I looked at the activated fire gem in the hearth next to Mother's plush reading chair in the corner. The ruby had gone from its dark red to a blood orange as the fire within burned indefinitely.

I then moved my eyes back to the display table. Next to Grandmother's first invention was a large metal box containing a few force gems and fire gems. With the help of the same lord who collaborated with the fire gems, Grandmother created something to provide heat to an entire home: the heat gem. Then after that rested the gem-comm, used for calling anyone from long distances, and the gem-image used for capturing still pictures. And then Grandmother's crowning achievement...

I stopped in front of the miniature model of the mage carriage that Oserans used regularly. The model was created from a square piece of iron, with a hood displaying where its force gems would reside, and four wheels at its sides. I picked up the model. It was heavy, but it fit entirely in my grip. Grandmother always said the one thing that would surpass the fire gem was when her mage carriage went into production.

"This is what will change Osera forever," she would say in her scratchy voice. I smiled, picturing her wrinkled, thin lips and a knobby, old finger twirling a white strand of hair on her head. She had always kept her hair long.

Of course, mage carriages were still hard to come by because the many large force gems used to power them were costly, as were the materials needed to create the machine itself. But Grandmother was still correct: though there was a lot of progress to be made, and many ideas had yet to come to fruition, her inventions began to pave the way for a new world. And Mother was intent on following in Grandmother's footsteps.

I placed the model back down and quickly glanced over all of Mother's inventions: the light gems, the blueprints for adding running water to homes, the plans for *heated* water, and the gem-motions for capturing *moving* images that Mother was in the process of creating by using Father's illusion Mage Gift. He could create any image in his mind and bring it to life. Of course, his creations weren't real, but they gave that appearance. He could make the illusions last as long as he had strength, and he could also make them *do* anything.

But Mother's crowning achievement: Her Mage Gift allowed her to make copies of her *own* ability. Our family was literally the owner and seller of the ability to invent and advance society and technology.

When Mother wasn't inventing new things herself, she made three special gems a day. These gems, called Melton gems, contained copies of her Gift within diamonds, and our family sold them. People used them to create their own machines and devices to progress the New Age. But she could only produce three a day, for diamonds were scarce.

The limited supply of the Melton gems, and all other inventions, made it so only the rich could afford such things. Mother hated that. Ideas were everywhere, and Mother was notorious for saying that the rich tended to be lazy, making the overall industrialization of Osera and elsewhere move too slowly.

I breathed heavily through my nose and placed a hand on the thin golden chain hanging from my neck. I froze as the feeling of the cold necklace against my fingers reminded me of the request I had for my parents before the party started.

"What time is it?" I exclaimed, whirling around to see my mother sitting atop her short stool with a nose pressed against some blueprints she had laid across her wide desk. She really needed to start wearing her spectacles. Age hadn't done much to her, but her vision was definitely a victim of the passing years.

"Yes, dear?"

I bit my lip. "Time, Mother. I asked for the time."

She squinted up at me, a blank look on her face as her thoughts were still on the plans before her.

I tapped my foot hurriedly, nodding my head at the silver timepiece strapped around her wrist.

"Oh!" She giggled and pulled her slender arm in front of her eyes. "Thirty minutes till. Are you nervous about the party?"

I wrung my hands together and shifted my eyes to my feet. "I was hoping to ask you and Father for another illusion necklace. You know, *for* the party. Just in case."

Mother rose from her stool, brow furrowed and lips pursed. "I think that's something you need to ask of your father."

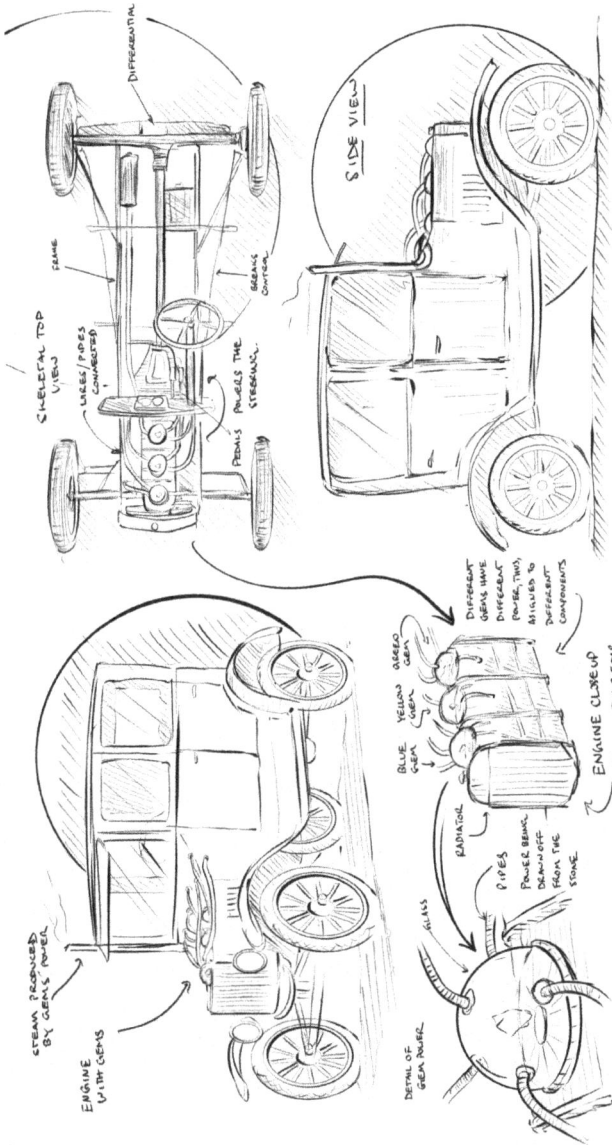

The labels on the blueprint read:

Skeletal top view: DIFFERENTIAL · FRAME · BRAKES CONTROL · LOCKS/PEDES CONNECTED · PEDALS POWERS THE STEERING

Side view: SIDE VIEW

Lower left carriage: STEAM PRODUCED BY GEMS POWER · ENGINE WITH GEMS

Engine closeup: DIFFERENT GEMS HAVE DIFFERENT POWER, THUS, MIXING TO DIFFERENT COMPONENTS · GREEN GEM · BLUE YELLOW GEM · ENGINE CLOSE UP POWER BY GEMS · RADIATOR · PIPES · POWER BEING DRAWN OFF FROM THE STONE · GLASS · DETAIL OF GEM POWER

The First Blueprint of the Mage Carriage

3

Julie

THE DISTANCE FROM MOTHER'S STUDY TO FATHER'S
was great. After stumbling through three long corri-
dors in the ridiculous nude-colored heels Mother
had bought me for the party, I finally stopped to
kick them off and scooped them into my grip.

I reached Father's massive mahogany door and
raised a knuckle to knock but was interrupted by
the sound of arguing. I held my breath and shrank
away.

"But the immigrants, especially those from Ish-
forsaken Ufith, are causing the problem! Before you
know it, there will be more half-breeds and ungifted

than we can control." I recognized Uncle Morris's gruff voice. "Immigration needs to come to a stop, and tariffs need to continue rising. We don't want to encourage Aloya to advance. Who knows? They might want to attack just as Ufith tried four years ago!"

I winced. I'd always known Uncle Morris felt strongly against the ungifted. Non-Oserans, and even Oserans with Gifts that didn't benefit society; they were just a nuisance to him. That was one among the many reasons my parents and I decided long ago not to inform Morris of my lack of a Gift.

Still, I loved Uncle Morris, ever since the day he first carried me on his shoulders when I was a little girl. He would run with me down the hallways, all the while ignoring Father and Mother's cries for him to stop running indoors. But even with all the good memories, it was hard to feel comfortable around him. If he knew my secret, what would he think of his perfect niece then?

And secondly, he loved politics. I did not. It was hard to form my own opinions about such topics, especially with the contention politics brought after the war. Mother was decidedly against many ideas of the New Age, a period most people saw as the time for societal and technological advancements. Of course, she was all for advancement, but many of the new philosophies and politics irked her. Mother was open about her views, but Father always seemed neutral. Or he just didn't voice his opinion. I didn't know enough of the world outside of home to make my own decisions yet.

"Calm down, Morris," Father said in his deep, nonthreatening voice.

"The Supreme Minister agrees with me!" Uncle Morris snapped.

"Well, I didn't vote for him." Again, Father was the calm one. He was always the peacemaker, just like his wife.

I heard the exasperated sigh from Morris through the still-closed door.

"Don't forget that I am your elder brother, Herbert. You shouldn't speak to me that way."

"Morris, if you don't like my opinions, then don't ask for them."

A small smile crept onto my thin lips. Even I knew that Morris needed a little chiding from his younger, and frequently wiser, brother Herbert Melton.

My thoughts distracted me so much that I didn't notice the sound of the knob turning and Uncle Morris's heavy footfalls as he huffed out of Father's study. The short man mumbled with his head down and stormed in my direction. I noticed too late and failed to dodge him. Uncle Morris ran right into me, his balding head bouncing off my shoulder.

"Ish!" he hissed, rubbing his head.

I cringed at the use of his favorite swear word: Ish, King of the Void, the devil.

My cheeks grew warm as Uncle Morris attempted to regain his composure. His round face glowed red, and bits of sweat fell into his dark brows.

"So sorry, Uncle! I was just on my way to see Father." I did not mention my eavesdropping.

A grin lit up Morris's ruddy face. "Julie! How's my favorite niece?"

I smiled back. Morris had two nieces, my sister and me, but I knew he was serious when he said I was his favorite. Our shared fervor for reading, the outdoors, and living life brought about a special comradery we had with no one else.

But even with all of that, it was hard not to tense up as he studied me with his large eyes. Any day, any *minute*, he could find out what I'd been hiding from him and the rest of the world.

I smacked my lips to add moisture to my suddenly dry mouth, then squeaked out, "Just trying to get through today."

Uncle Morris fondly grabbed my hands. "You'll do great, Julie. And Calvin seems like a wonderful man."

My heart jumped and my face felt flush at the mention of my betrothed's name. I'd only had two interactions with Calvin Sexton thus far. He was the only child of the lording family that presided over Pirbis South. My family led Pirbis North, the capital of Osera, but Pirbis South was almost equal to the north in size and wealth. So, when Mother and Father suggested him as a match to me, they stressed heavily why such a marriage would benefit the entire country.

Morris must have noticed my face reddening, and he nudged me with an elbow.

"He's a handsome one, eh?" he teased.

I rubbed the back of my neck and dipped my chin. "Yes, very handsome."

And he was. Handsome, taller than me (finally), and incredibly charming. I grew lightheaded just thinking back to the day prior when one of our two interactions took place: the way he offered a hand to me as we strolled the manor grounds together and the genuine questions and interest he'd shown to my parents. Many said Calvin Sexton was lucky to marry a Melton, the Meltons being the country's most powerful and richest lording family. Still, I almost felt *I* was the lucky one to have someone like Calvin marry *me*.

Morris took my silence as an end to our conversation and gave my hands a little squeeze.

"I have to get back to the jail before your party starts." He pulled out a silver pocket watch from his inside suit pocket and grimaced at it. "Not much time, huh?"

With a quick nod of goodbye, Uncle Morris went on his way. I shivered. I didn't know how *I* would feel if I had become the warden of Pirbis North Prison rather than inheriting the Melton estate as my father did. But Morris didn't show remorse or hostility toward his younger brother—at least not often.

Besides, it was almost as if Morris was *born* for his job. His Gift allowed him to strip others of theirs, and his primary role was to do this to the prisoners. And if you ended up in Pirbis North Prison, rest assured Morris would strip you of your Gift. It was the law, and the Supreme Minister was pushing for gems with Morris's Gift to be made, allowing this stripping to happen to criminals throughout Osera.

It felt weird to even think about Uncle Morris's job when it was a forbidden topic around my mother. The utilization of his Gift on every criminal, no matter how big or small their offense, was one of the many things she and her brother-in-law disagreed upon.

Attempting to calm my nerves, I flexed my fingers, then closed them over and over again and settled my breathing. I straightened my shoulders, pushed the door open, and stepped into Father's study.

Unlike Mother's, the room where Father worked was spacious. His marble hearth was twice as large as hers and used a second fire gem rather than the usual one. Father had two leather sitting chairs, one in each corner at the end of the room, and the simple, gray rug on the floor stretched at least twenty feet.

"Ah, Julie. You are a sight for sore eyes."

I raised my gaze to meet Father's. He sat at his long, mahogany desk, fingers clasped atop it. His shoulders were straight as an arrow, and the muscles in his arms flexed as he leaned toward me. If I had to conclude which parent I looked more like, it would be him. Other than the height from Mother, nearly everything else came from Father's gene pool: the blue eyes, the thick, dark brown hair.

Father smiled at me from underneath his neat beard. I tried to return the smile, but my nerves returned. I shifted my eyes back to my shuffling feet.

"What is it?" he said. Without looking at him, I could almost feel him frowning just by the sound of his voice.

I gulped but decided to get it over with: "Father, you know the party is happening tonight."

"Of course."

I chuckled slightly. "Yes, of course. I was

hoping... Well, I think I *need* another illusion necklace."

The reclining chair Father sat upon creaked as he pushed his body back into it. I bit my lip and peeked a single eye up at him. The wrinkles in his face deepened as his frown grew.

"Oh, Julie. You know you don't actually *need* them. I love you, your mother loves you, Eliza loves you. Whether you have a Mage Gift or not, you're still our darling Julie."

I wrung my hands. I knew he'd say that. Both Mother and Father had spoken against the farce from the beginning. I never had a Mage Gift. And after years of trying to find it, I finally gave up. But even if Othos chose not to bestow a Gift upon me, he still gave me some of the most powerful parents in history. My father had his incredible illusion Gift, and my mother could copy and store his Gift in any gem. And that is how my idea came to fruition.

Mother and Father would make me objects that I could use to apply illusions to myself. Mage Gifts were often inherited, so it made sense that I would have a Gift similar to Father's. Just four years ago, as I crept closer to turning twenty, the age one typically marries, I was put into more social environments. It made me increasingly nervous, so I decided necklaces were the perfect objects for Mother and Father to make—necklaces with gems encrusted in the chains, or hidden at the back of pendants that, once activated, would turn me into a completely different person. At least, I would have the *illusion* that I was someone else. As long as I had an activated necklace on my person, I could sustain the image as long as I wished.

I had a necklace that transformed me into Father, Mother, my sister Eliza, Morris, half of the manor's serving staff, and even a few local officials. And necklaces were perfect, for I would use them at events, galas, or any public appearance to ward off any unwanted questions about what my Mage Gift was. Or—Othos forbid—if I even had one.

"Do you not have enough of the necklaces?" Father's sorrowful voice interrupted my thoughts.

"What if someone at the party has seen all my illusions? I might get caught!" I blurted, fists clenched at my sides.

Father rubbed his face with his large hands and sighed. "It's in the cabinet behind you. Top drawer."

I froze. "Y—you already made one?"

He shrugged. "I knew you would want one." His moist and wide eyes met mine. "I just want you to be happy, dear."

My parents didn't worry about the scandal that would ensue if word got out that the Meltons had a daughter with no Mage Gift. But they were wrong to feel that way. Either I was one of those rare anomalies, which was strange and unheard of, or I was a bastard. It would cause too much unwanted attention. I had to keep up the farce, and I insisted my parents had to continue going along with it.

I cocked my head in a thank you to my father and slowly turned toward the cabinet. It was tall, nearly reaching the ceiling. The top drawer scraped open as I pulled its brass knob. Inside a compartment at the back, I saw something sparkle. I reached in and felt a cold chain.

I pulled out the piece of jewelry to admire it in a better light. Tiny, silver links made up a long chain and led to a shining emerald pendant. I frowned. I didn't typically like to wear necklaces with the gem in plain sight. Gems were scarce and in high demand to run machines, so some people were offended by the wealthy wearing gems for something as useless as jewelry. Sometimes my parents would hide illusion gems in a locket for my necklaces or decorate the chain with smaller, less obvious gems.

"I know the emerald is large, but your mother and I thought it would be good for you to wear something nice for your engagement party."

Father was right. It was nice. Despite the disdain for necklaces or rings sporting precious stones, an equal number of wealthy people wouldn't attend an event without one. People's legitimate need for

49

gems made them all the more valuable. That increased the rich's desire to add a gem to their ensemble.

My heart warmed at my parents' good intentions. It truly showed how much they cared for me to have the best night possible. I ran a finger over the emerald. I could almost feel the Mage Gift stored within tingling onto my skin. I smiled, pulled the simple gold necklace I'd been wearing all day off my neck, then replaced it with the new design.

"Thank you, Father. It's beautiful," I said.

Father nodded, a soft smile creeping on his lips. He really *did* seek his daughter's happiness.

"You know, Julie. I read something last night where someone found their Mage Gift after giving birth to their first-born. And you're to be wed soon."

I palmed my forehead. He meant well. He really did. And yes, some Oserans born without Gifts were just late-bloomers who had to find the right conditions to activate the ability. But almost no one lasted as long as I without finding said condition. And I tried *everything*, all the while hoping that I just needed to do some strange thing to secure my Gift. I ate a bug when I was six years old, I purposely burned my hand on a fire gem at nine, and once I even tried jumping out of a second-story window. The broken ankle that ensued had just been embarrassing.

"You're only saying that because you want grandkids," I suggested.

Father shrugged and tried to hide the smile on his face. "There was a time you were searching *everywhere* for stories and ideas to help activate your Gift."

He was right. But after many years of trying, all the ideas we could conjure began to sound ridiculous.

"I'll see you at the party," I said with a wave.

~

THERE IT WAS. The giant double doors opened before me and allowed a flood of bright yellow light to spill from the grand ballroom, warming my face. Guests were to arrive any minute, and final preparations continued within. The staff bustled about, making sure the maroon-colored cloths over the dozen long tables were straight, then placing the multitude of dinner courses, desserts, and champagne at each place setting.

My mouth watered at the sight of the food. I chuckled nervously as my stomach growled. At least one positive existed for having this engagement party: the excuse to have a feast.

Taking a deep breath, I reached a heeled shoe over the threshold to enter, but a gentle tap on my shoulder stopped me. I tipped my head to the side to see its source. My shoulders slumped in relief to see the delicate, round face of my sister beaming up at me.

"Oh, Eliza." I nearly toppled her over with my hug. My arms grasped Eliza's shoulders, and hers wrapped around just below my waist. Eliza was the spitting image of my mother, save for the short stature she received from Father.

"You're growing up so much, Julie."

I hadn't noticed my brother-in-law until he spoke. Eliza's husband had not been a part of any lording family before meeting my sister, but upon their nuptials, he and Eliza became heirs to the Melton fortune, and he received the title of Marquess Fletcher. Rumors abounded that John married with greedy intentions, but I knew better: He and my sister had simply fallen in love.

Eliza and I retracted from our embrace, and I gave a warm smile to the marquess. "Hello, John. It's so good to see you both."

The marquess approached his wife's side and wrapped a long arm around her narrow shoulders. He squeezed her briefly, but the movement was tense—almost as if he were holding her just for show.

At the beginning of their marriage, they had

been happy. But years passed, the war happened, and John changed.

I shook my head, trying to convince myself I had imagined it. I'd hoped the next time I saw them their relationship would be better. Still, it was a good sign to see them at the manor together.

By Othos' name, has it really been a year *since John and Eliza visited?*

John's years at the war had dragged the two of them away for a while—John at the front lines and Eliza trying to live as close to her husband as possible. That made their visits few and far between.

I reached out for Eliza's dainty hands and squeezed them in my own. Oh, how I missed her and the adventures we shared. Only three years my senior, Eliza was my confidante in everything. I thought fondly back to whispering to a nine-year-old Eliza about my first crush: Patrick Samson—a cute, ruddy-faced little boy from grade school.

"We can catch up after the party," Eliza whispered as she winked. "People are beginning to arrive."

My breathing grew shallow as I noticed the swarm of chattering people approaching us.

I gulped. "Yes, I'll see you then."

4

Julie

"A TOAST TO THE LORD AND LADY MELTON, BUT especially to the bride-to-be and her handsome groom!"

Cheers and the clinking sounds of champagne flutes erupted around me as Uncle Morris made the first toast. I warily raised my glass, beads of water already forming on the outside of the cold cup and wetting my fingers. I forced a nervous smile and took a sip. The pleasant, nutty flavor slid its way down my throat, and I happily took another swallow—*longer* this time.

Uncle Morris laughed jovially from across the

long table. Then he downed his own glass much too fast.

I dared a look to my right to watch as my fiancé, Calvin, laughed along with the guests. He seemed so comfortable with the situation. Like he was in his element.

The sound of hushed bickering just past Calvin's seat snapped me out of my reverie. I flashed a look at Eliza and John and saw him leaning close and hissing at her through gritted teeth.

Although Eliza had many physical similarities to my mother, she lacked Mother's confident air. Eliza's demure personality often made it easy for her angry husband to trample all over her.

My sister's soft pink lips trembled as her giant husband quietly snapped at her. But what was he so frustrated about?

Oh, Eliza, I thought, *it's still happening?*

My hopes dimmed for their marriage growing happier as John's temper seemed to flare up just inches away from me. John Fletcher had been kind once. But then the war happened, and the brutality of it had calloused him.

I watched solemnly as Eliza insisted the two of them leave so as not to interrupt the party.

"It's Julie's day," I heard her whisper. "Let's talk about this somewhere else."

Without a glance in Eliza's direction, John

huffed toward the closest exit. Eliza took a deep breath, nervously smiled at each of us, and hurried away after her husband.

I made a point to look in Father's direction. He chewed on the inside of his cheek and glared at his son-in-law's back. Father knew of his daughter's marital problems, and he didn't like the marquess because of them.

"Are they going to be alright?"

I started at the touch of Calvin's fingers brushing my elbow. I turned to him, face growing hot.

"Oh, yes. I'm sure they will be."

Calvin smiled. It was a charmingly crooked smile, and I could have sworn I saw a twinkle in his eye.

"I think the dancing has started." He gestured to a spot amid all the tables. A few couples had started dancing to the slow, rhythmic music played by the brass instruments behind us. "Would you like to join me on the floor?"

My shoulders relaxed. His silvery voice calmed me. I took Calvin's outstretched hand and allowed him to lead me away from the table and among the other dancing couples.

Calvin stopped in front of me. I didn't quite have to crane my neck up to look into his face, but he still had a couple of inches on me. My heart fluttered as he delicately placed one hand on my waist and brought my arm up with his as we positioned ourselves to move to the music.

Calvin set his strong, square jaw and closed his eyes, focusing intently on the rhythm and moving gracefully across the wooden floor and in between couples. I took the opportunity to study him.

His chiseled cheeks glowed from the light of many glass chandeliers hanging about the grand ballroom. His chestnut hair was just long enough that it fell in front of his alluring, light-green eyes, obscuring his view of me as I stared. He truly was handsome. Almost too much so.

I didn't know much about my betrothed. Only that he was twenty-nine—five years older than I—and his father had unexpectedly passed away just the year prior. And he was endearing. Something bewildered me about Lord Sexton; perhaps it was his gentleness toward me. People acquainted with him said they took pride in knowing him.

Calvin's strong arms swept me into a wide turn, and I giggled as my shoes slid across the floor. But I trusted him. I felt safe in his grip.

"You look beautiful tonight," he said.

I shifted my eyes downward, grinning uncontrollably. "Really? There's nothing you would change? Even with your Mage Gift?"

Calvin's Mage Gift was interesting. He inherited the ability from his mother, which was the Gift to change color pigmentation on any face instantaneously. Lady Sexton could change eye color or add pretty pinks and reds to someone's cheeks and lips. But Calvin's Gift went a step further: Lord Sexton could make minor tweaks and changes to your physical features. He could make a nose trimmer, eyelashes longer... Of course, it was only temporary. The physical changes came off when washed away —just like makeup.

He threw his head back and laughed. "The changes I could make to your face would be completely unnecessary. Besides, if you wanted to change yourself, I think you have that covered."

My eyes flickered down to my neck, where the illusion necklace rested. I knew he referred to my Mage Gift. How could I possibly continue deceiving him? Would I always pretend to have a Mage Gift around him? Would he even want me if he knew the truth?

Before I could stumble out a reply, Calvin stepped away and gave me a polite nod.

"If you will excuse me for a moment, Miss Julie. There is someone in attendance that wishes to meet with me. But I will find your company again shortly."

Flustered, I nodded back and watched as he stepped away and disappeared among the masses.

"Hello, Miss Julie."

I whirled around to see a party guest standing behind me. The old man's hands were clasped behind his back, and he flashed me a toothy grin. I looked down. I was used to being on the taller side, but this man's head barely reached my shoulder.

"Ah, Lord…"

"Lord Thompson." He gave me a swooping bow. I winced at the sound of his back cracking as he did. "At your service, milady."

I hesitantly allowed the Lord to take my hand and plant a wet kiss on my knuckles. It took everything in me to plaster a smile on my face and not allow a scowl to come through.

Without even asking—wait, had he asked?—Lord Thompson pulled me into a dance as the musicians started another song.

The lord wasn't musically inclined like my betrothed. Lord Thompson trod on my toes more than once; his movements were quite awkward and offbeat. The man's lack of height made it so I could see the other guests snickering at the old man.

"If I may trouble you, my dear," Lord Thompson chirped over the music, "would you be willing to show me a little taste of your Mage Gift? Your family is legendary, and I have a particular interest in your father's Gift."

My heart dropped to my stomach. Of course, that's what he wanted. That's what they *all* wanted.

But it was more than just my Gift; he wanted to see a *Melton* Gift. We were famous. Even though Lord Thompson might know many others who had just as spectacular a Gift as Father's, it was merely our reputation. If only Father and Mother could see this exchange, then they would know the necessity of my illusion necklaces.

I slammed my teeth down on my tongue, attempting to use the pain to distract from the sudden sick feeling to my stomach. Each time I was asked to display my Gift, the greater the chance I would unintentionally tarnish the family name.

"Certainly," I replied, already moving to discreetly tap the side of my necklace's pendant to activate it.

I planned on displaying my "Gift" at some point during the party, and sooner rather than later was good, I presumed. I just hoped Laura's friend, the new maid, had a decent view of my show so I wouldn't have to do it all over again.

But before my finger made contact, Lord Thompson twirled in a circle and addressed the crowd: "The bride-to-be is about to showcase her Mage Gift!"

I gulped, noticing every single eye in the room was on me. My limbs trembled at the sound of excited gasps, then the eruption of applause. I felt one gaze in particular boring into me sorrowfully as the party guests urged me to display my Gift.

I met eyes with my mother. She still sat at the head of our family's dinner table. She gave me a short shake of her head, making the pearls that hung from her ears hit the sides of her neck.

I have to, I thought to her, as if she could hear the words in my head. Mother merely shifted her eyes away and continued to chat with an elderly woman adorning what was an apparent orange wig atop her head.

Mother, I was sure, didn't want me to flaunt my lies. Father would disapprove, as well. Wait— Where was Father? He was no longer sitting beside Mother, and a quick scan of the ballroom offered no further sight of him. Had he gone to check on Eliza? Father was often trying to help my sister with her unhealthy marriage.

"Come on, Miss Julie," Lord Thompson prodded with a clumsy wink. "We're waiting."

"Do me!" a shrill voice cried.

"No, my daughter!" another contributed.

Realization struck me in the gut as my stomach flipped. I had forgotten to ask Father to whom the necklace would transform me. I provided a shy smile to the crowd.

"Isn't the fun in the surprise?" I suggested.

I know I'll *be surprised.*

While the guests laughed, I slyly tapped my finger on the button at the side of the emerald.

As usual, I didn't see or feel the change. The hallucination activated within seconds, and I knew a new image covered me merely by the looks on the guests' faces. Jaws dropped, and more applause sounded. My smile twitched treacherously as I tried to look for any clues on the awestruck faces as to whom I had transformed.

"Ah, Supreme Minister Harold." Lord Thompson gave me another one of his back-cracking bows. "It's an honor to have you in our company." He chuckled along with the rest of the crowd.

"I thought you would all like it," I croaked as a pit formed in my stomach. If only their praise could apply to something I could genuinely do.

~

I STROLLED the halls by myself, just as I had earlier that day. I was happy to have escaped from the dancing, the chatting, and all the attention directed on me—even if my escape would be brief. I knew Mother would send someone after me shortly, so I tried to cherish my solitude while I could.

I stopped at the end of the corridor and rested my head on the wall and closed my eyes against the few light gems providing dim light. Most of the light gems had been moved to the grand ballroom to illuminate the dinner party.

"I am so tired of your father meddling in our affairs!"

The shouting came from behind a slightly opened, bright white door with yellow sunflowers painted along the edges—the entrance to one of Mother's *many* libraries. I recognized the gravelly voice of my brother-in-law immediately and shrank into a corner covered by shadows.

"Who is *he* to say what we do or don't do with your Gift? What you inherited from your mother is more valuable than you can possibly imagine!" John raised his voice again, but soon the conversing returned to whispers.

I inched closer to hear better, trying to ignore the voice in my head that eavesdropping twice in one day wasn't the best idea. I was too curious to avoid listening in. What did John want to do with Eliza's Gift? She had inherited the store-and-copy ability from our mother. However, she'd never shown interest in pursuing a life revolving around her Gift as our mother had. Did John want to make money off of Eliza's Gift? Did he have a device in mind he wanted his wife to create for him?

Drawing a deep breath, I peeked through the doorway. First, I saw John's bright red hair glinting from the glow of a fire gem in the middle of the library. And Eliza sat in a brown armchair underneath the shadow of her husband as he stood over her.

Her dainty face portrayed a blank expression. Her full lips were pressed into a straight line, and her stormy eyes stared off at a far corner rather than gazing up at her husband.

"You can't talk to me like that, John," she whispered.

My brother-in-law straightened his back and clenched his pale fists. "What did you say?"

Eliza flashed her eyes up at him suddenly. The look of anger and fire within them startled me so much I almost gasped. But I bit my tongue and continued to watch.

"I said," she snapped, raising her voice, "you can't talk to me that way! Not to me, and not to my father!"

My jaw dropped. I had never seen Eliza talk back to John, much less *anyone*, with such bravery.

Eliza rose from her chair and placed a steady hand on her belly. "The person you have become, John, is *not* the person I want raising our child."

This time, the gasp slipped from my lips.

I threw a hand to my mouth once I realized the sound I had made and squinted my eyes shut, embarrassed, as John and Eliza turned toward me.

John's face flushed a crimson as we met eyes. His red beard bounced up and down as he opened his mouth over and over to say something, but no words came out. He shifted his eyes to his feet and retreated from Eliza.

Eliza gave me a faltering smile. "John," she said, stepping away and toward me, "I will see you shortly."

"Sorry," I mouthed to her.

Eliza shook her head, the smile remaining on her pretty face, but a single tear escaped her eye and trickled down her pink cheeks.

"Come, Julie," she said, grabbing the crook of my arm and directing me away. "Let's allow John to cool off a bit." Eliza whipped her head around, her long blond curls smacking my cheek. "I'm warning you, John. I will not allow you to push me around any longer."

We left the little library, and the heavy door shut behind us with a loud *bang*.

"Eliza! You stood up to him! That was amazing!" I looked down at my sister's belly and felt warmth grow inside of me. "And you're *pregnant*? I had no idea!"

Eliza dropped my arm and stared down at the floor. What had once been a single tear was now a multitude of them. The droplets spilled past her nose and hit the white carpet at our feet.

"Eliza?" I moved to rest a comforting hand on her shoulder, but Eliza backed away from me. Her eyes veered over my shoulder at something behind me.

"What?" I urged. "What is it?"

I turned my head to see where Eliza was staring. The maid Laura peeked her head around the wall. I had run into her a lot in just one day. But where had she been hiding? Had she been listening in on the arguing, too?

"I—I—I'm sorry, missus," she stuttered, scurrying away. Her strawberry-blond curls bounced after her.

I looked back at Eliza, worried she would feel embarrassed of Laura having witnessed her argument with John.

"I just—I need to be alone for a little while," Eliza stammered.

Before I could reply, Eliza turned on her heel and sped away. I frowned, debating whether it was worth chasing after her.

I exhaled heavily through my nose and decided it was best to return to the party.

5

John

JOHN FLETCHER FELT LIKE A WRETCHED FOOL FOR how he treated his wife. And it was happening much more often than it used to. Even as he yelled or fumed at Eliza and her family, he *knew* it was a terrible thing to do.

John sat against one of the many tall bookcases in the library. Hundreds of books surrounded him, too many to finish in his lifetime. He often wondered why Lady Melton needed six libraries in the manor.

John put his face into his knees and began to sob. What had the war done to him? He used to be a patient, loving man. Now, all he felt was hatred and anger. It was a constant, and it was exhausting.

After a few moments of tears, the marquess rose from the floor and strode over to the hearth. The warmth from the fire gems dried his tear-stained cheeks. John stood by the heat for a moment, thinking of his beautiful wife and the baby within her.

John loved Eliza—he always had. He hadn't married her because she was a Melton, and not even because of her Mage Gift. From the moment he'd set eyes on her, John had fallen in love with her radiant beauty and generous heart. And then the war happened.

Ufith, a far-off monarchist continent to the east, declared war on the world of Dagirus. The king of Eshor, one of Ufith's countries, had taken over the rest of his continent and moved to take all others, including Osera. King Gerald was jealous of Oseran advancements, as his people lacked Mage Gifts and the ability to industrialize and grow. His empire was mostly desert with few resources to trade for any inventions, so King Gerald instead declared war in an effort to control Oseran advancement.

Fearing a dictatorship and tyranny ruling the world, Oserans pushed for an alliance with Aloya— another, more peaceful monarchist continent—and held Ufith back.

After decades without any need for large army forces, Oseran Supreme Minister Harold created a draft, a lottery to select from men between eighteen and forty. And thirty-two-year old John Fletcher's name was picked.

John paced the length of the library, kicking aside the wool rug under his feet. John squinted his eyes nearly shut as he paced, remembering the shooting from the force canes of Osera, the swords and spears of the more primitive Aloya and Ufith armies, the screams... And he remembered his own force-cane in his hands with its glowing force gem and the power it wielded when pointed at enemies' hearts—not like the shorter canes policemen were given to stun assailants' limbs, making them immobile for a short time. The ones John and many others used in the war stunned hearts, which instantly killed the enemy soldier.

Every time he had looked upon the cane while at the front lines, he thought of two things: His wife's grandmother, who had aided in inventing such weapons, and the lives he'd taken with the machine.

John shuddered and threw himself into the armchair Eliza had been resting in just moments before.

If only I had never gone to war, he thought, head resting in the palms of his hands.

A creaking sound of the library door opening interrupted John from his thoughts. He raised his head slowly, wiping away any stray tears from his hairy face.

"Yes?" he said to the darkness. John peered past the shadows in an attempt to see who had entered.

The door closed shut behind the figure, and John could hear the click of a woman's heeled shoes on the wooden floor.

John blinked quickly, trying to adjust his eyes to the dim lighting after having pressed his face into his hands.

"Who's there?" he demanded.

The newcomer emerged from the darkness, and the orange glow of the fire gem lit up one side of her face.

"Eliza?" John leaped up from his chair and rushed over to his wife. "I'm so sorry. I didn't—"

Eliza Melton had a strange smile on her face. Her white teeth glinted from the moonlight shining through the single window in the room.

John placed a hand on her face and scooped his head downward to look directly into her steady eyes.

"Eliza, are you alright? You seem—"

John was interrupted as he saw the shine of something silver. He looked down at Eliza's hand and gasped as he saw a short knife clutched in her grip, knuckles turning white from grasping it tightly.

"Eliza!" he cried out, stumbling backward and raising his hands up in defense. "What has gotten into you?"

His wife shifted the knife in her hand as she began to finger the simple, leather hilt with a certain fervor. Eliza approached, her light eyebrows raised as her grin widened.

"Please, my love," he cried, but she didn't stop.

∼

"I. Have. To. Tell. Them," John spat through gritted teeth, shakily clutching at his bleeding chest. The warm blood seeped through his fingers; he knew he only had seconds.

With a loud groan, John flipped himself onto his stomach. He inched his way over the rug and to a section of the hardwood floor. His vision turned red as the agonizing pain tore through his body.

"Almost. There," he gasped, a bloodied finger poised above the floor.

With his final seconds, the former soldier wrote a few letters in his own blood. But before he could finish, John felt the final pang of his fresh stab wound, and his lifeless head collapsed on top of his last message.

~

Julie

I WATCHED the couples twirl away on the dance floor late into the night. I rested my chin in my palm, elbow propped up on our family's table. Even Mother was dancing, but by herself. I smiled as she waved her arms gracefully to the music and tapped her feet with the rhythm. Mother always loved a good party. But where was Father?

Mother stopped dancing and flashed a brilliant smile in my direction. She threw her head back and let out a loud, melodious laugh, then waved me over. My breath caught.

"No," I mouthed to her with a quick shake of my head.

Mother proceeded to firmly plant her hands on her hips. "Come *on*," she mouthed back.

I released a long breath of air and slowly pushed my chair away from the table. I knew better than to deny Mother more than once. Shoulders slumped, and eyes avoiding others, I made my way to Mother. She grasped my hands in hers and spun us in about a dozen circles in rhythm to the fast-paced music.

I couldn't help but giggle as we spun and

weaved our way through the guests like little schoolgirls. But our footsteps stumbled as the music stopped, and we lurched forward as we fell near a group of men chatting with each other. Mother nearly landed on the brown leather shoes of one of the gentlemen, but she caught herself just in time. I wasn't so lucky:

I banged my nose straight into the shoulder of another man, but his strong arms caught me in his grip before I tumbled to the floor.

"Whoa, there, Julie."

I sighed in relief at the sound of Uncle Morris's voice, then straightened myself and gave him a quick, embarrassed nod. He bit a lip to keep from laughing at us.

"We are so, so sorry!" Mother gasped with a few chuckles. She clutched a hand to her chest as she tried to catch her breath. "Our feet got away from us for a moment there."

"Yes," I added, my face growing uncomfortably warm. I didn't feel as amused by the mistake as Mother did. "So sorry."

Three men made up the group, one Uncle Morris and the other two I didn't recognize. One of the strangers seemed to be in his thirties, and the other was at least sixty.

"Oh, don't worry about it," Morris said with a wave of his hand.

He winked at me but avoided looking in my mother's direction. The two of them seldom spoke with one another. Sure, they disagreed on many political topics, but there was something deeper. My uncle's entire body seemed to cave in on itself whenever Mother approached—like he was in some sort of pain.

"Yes, no worries at all," the elderly man said, raising his glass cheerfully. He sniffed so hard after taking a sip, it made his gray beard bobble up and down. "I wanted to meet the Mother of Modernity, anyway." He gave a stiff bow to Mother. "*And* her lovely daughter."

Mother flushed at the use of her nickname. All of Osera seemed to use it. While Grandmother had been known as the "Mother of Invention," my mother's nickname stemmed from being the one who truly paved the way for Osera to enter the New Age, especially when it came to technological advancement.

"Oh, please," Mother whispered with a flutter of her long eyelashes, "no need for that name here."

"I have to agree with Lord Peele," the younger man said with a crooked smile. He had a deep scar stretching across what must have once been a handsome face. "It is great to meet two of the legendary Melton women."

The scarred man looked at me. Our height was

about the same, and I could tell that made him slightly uncomfortable as his brown eyes studied me.

"And congratulations to you, Miss Melton," he said.

"Wait, are you John's friend? From the war?" Mother thrust a hand out to shake his.

The man laughed a little and took her hand. "Yes, Eugene Branch. And we weren't exactly *friends*, but our paths crossed every once in a while."

I felt a tap on my shoulder and jumped about a foot in the air, making the men in front of me raise their brows. I gave a nervous smile and turned to see the newcomer.

"I didn't mean to scare you." Calvin's smooth voice calmed me as he pulled my hand into his to kiss it. My heart fluttered, and I brought my free hand up to my face to cover my red cheeks.

"So sorry to interrupt, gentlemen, but may I steal my beautiful fiancée?"

The men gave various grunts of approval, and Morris winked at me. Calvin offered his arm. I took it and gratefully allowed him to lead me away from the conversation.

At the dinner table, Calvin pulled a wooden chair across the floor and gestured for me to sit. I beamed up at my fiancé and followed his instruction. He took an empty chair to my left and prof-fered a glass of champagne.

"I thought you would like some refreshment."

I stared at the thin glass in his hand and felt a craving for the alcohol. I graciously accepted the drink and took a few dainty sips.

And then I heard a scream.

6

Julie

THE LITTLE LIBRARY WAS SO CROWDED I COULD NOT tell whose body lay on the floor. Panic ensued as more guests and servants rushed into the little library. "Who is it?" a woman whispered. The room smelled of sweat, tears, and the metallic scent of blood—a scent I only knew from scraping my knees as a child, pricking my finger on a rose bush, and witnessing the manor chef accidentally slide a cooking knife across her bare skin. But I had never smelled blood as I did at that moment—it was strong, and there must have been a lot of it.

"A murder! Who could ever believe such a thing?" another murmured.

My lip trembled as I anxiously craned my head back and forth to get a better view of the body. All I could see was a bloodied hand with a pool of more blood beside it stretching across and staining Mother's favorite rug. I concurred with the last voice: I could never believe a *murder* would happen in my own home.

Calvin stood next to me, his almond-shaped eyes growing wide. "God of Beginnings," he prayed in a low voice, "Oh, Othos, bless his soul."

My body warmed at the sound of his prayer. I reached over and took his hand in my own, shocking myself. I could feel Calvin's limbs freeze in surprise, but they just as quickly softened as he flashed a grateful smile in my direction. He squeezed my hand, and my heart skipped a beat.

"What is the meaning of this?"

Father pushed his way past Calvin and me and through the rest of the crowd, making a pathway directly to the body. I gasped once I finally saw who it was.

John Fletcher, my brother-in-law, lay in a puddle of blood and sweat. His face was smashed against the wood floor, and his lifeless, green eyes were still open.

I brought my free hand to my mouth, terror

ripping through me. I began to feel faint, but Calvin tightened his grip on my other hand, bringing me back to my surroundings.

"Is that...the marquess?" he whispered.

I replied only with a nod, unable to tear my eyes away from John's crumpled body.

Father cried out in horror and rushed over to his son-in-law. Kneeling beside the body, he ran his hands above John's torso, unsure of what to do.

"Who did this?" he stormed. I had never seen my father so angry.

And that is when the last two arrivals saw the scene.

"John?" Eliza cried.

"Oh, my..." Mother said, her face going from a healthy tan glow to a pale white.

Eliza threw herself across the room and sat directly next to Father. "No!"

"Julie," Father said.

I snapped to attention.

"Call the police."

I nodded, rushing over to the armchair in the library and fumbling my hands over the little table sitting next to it until I had a firm hold on the gem-comm atop it. Still shaking, I turned the five numbers associated with the police station: five, five, one, six, three.

Or, wait, is the last number a two?

Apologizing to the entire room, I redialed the correct number and held the cold earpiece to my ear and raised the heavy speaker to my mouth.

The room fell utterly silent. All of the party guests—there were dozens—filled the room and bled out into the hallway to see the happenings first hand. The ringing of the gem-comm blazed through my ear, and I could tell the rest of the people in the library could hear as well, for they leaned further forward with each ring.

"Pirbis North Police. What is your emergency?" The operator's voice sounded so calm and capable.

I gulped. "Uh, yes. This is Julie Melton of Melton Manor. We have a...a..." I squeezed my eyes shut and took a deep breath. "There seems to have been a murder."

∾

"HE'S DEAD, ALRIGHT."

The chief of police stood over John's body. He planted his hairy hands firmly on his hips and spread his feet shoulder's width apart. The chubby man looked a little ridiculous in his police uniform. It was the standard-issue deep blue with several pockets, a black belt for holding his badge and force cane, and many brass buttons lining the front. But the man's rolls bulged out of this uniform, a uniform likely made for him before all that extra weight appeared.

"But just for good measure..." The chief landed his right boot into John's ribs, which flipped the body over to its side and smeared the pools of blood across more of the floor.

"Excuse me!" Eliza shouted through her tears. "Show some respect!"

Mother moved from her position against the wall and rushed over to throw her arms around her eldest daughter's neck in a tight, protective embrace.

It was just Father, Mother, Eliza, three policemen, and me in the room. The chief had instructed all non-family guests to retreat to the grand ballroom under the careful watch of a few more of his men.

The chief—I think Marsh was his name—turned quickly on his heeled boot and pursed his lips as his blue eyes met Eliza's.

"I'm sorry, Miss Melton. Just have to make positive he's dead." The stubby man wiggled his long, curled mustache and turned back to the body. "And I needed to see the wound that caused the poor man's death."

Marsh bent into a squat with a great amount of effort as he studied John's tunic.

"Ah," he pointed a gloved finger at a spot to the left of his chest. "See where most of the blood on his shirt pooled right here? That must be the stab wound."

I shuddered. *Poor John.*

Eliza audibly whimpered once again and buried her face into Mother's shoulder.

"But who did it?" Father interjected. "Are you able to tell who committed this horrible crime?"

"If I may?"

We turned to the new voice. The serving maid Laura stood in the open doorway, wringing her hands. calloused from years of service at the manor. Her blue eyes darted nervously as she bent her head. Her red-gold hair fell over her nose as she did so.

"Yes, dear. What is it?" Marsh replied.

Laura said something, but it was so quiet we all leaned forward to try and hear better.

"Speak up, Laura," Father said calmly. "We couldn't quite hear that."

"I know who did it."

The silence that ensued overwhelmed everyone in the room. All jaws dropped, and my body stood frozen.

"Uh, well, that's great!" the chief said, clearing his throat. "And who did it?"

Laura glanced over in Eliza and Mother's direction. She bit her lip so hard I could see a drop of blood run down her chin.

"No," I breathed, "you can't mean—"

"It was Lady Fletcher," she blurted. Even as she said it, Laura slammed her hands over her mouth, almost ashamed of speaking at all.

"What?" Father cried.

Mother held her eldest daughter close to her chest protectively, and Eliza's face froze with shock. I knew I must have looked similar.

The two policemen standing in either corner at the end of the room reached for the force canes in their holsters and moved toward Eliza slowly, but Chief Marsh held up a hand to stop them.

"Wait," he said. He then directed his attention to Laura. "Are you sure?"

The woman had lost all the color to her cheeks, and she could barely nod in reply. "Yes. The missus was arguing with her husband right before his death. And she threatened him. Miss Julie saw, too."

All eyes landed on me, but I hadn't yet processed what Laura had said.

"Is that true?" Chief Marsh inquired of me.

My mouth went dry. "Uh, what?"

"Is it true you witnessed your sister and brother-in-law in a dispute? And did you hear Lady Fletcher threaten him?"

I warily looked over to my sister. Tears silently

spilled down her red cheeks. Her blonde hair, once pinned up neatly for the party, was now straggly and sticking up in various places. Her perfect pink lipstick had all but worn off, and her hands shook as she clung to our mother. I could never believe my sister would go so far as to kill anyone, much less her husband. She was the gentlest, sweetest person I'd ever known. But...

"I did," I answered.

Father groaned.

"But," I continued, "she didn't exactly threaten him."

"I beg your pardon, miss," Laura interjected, "but these were her exact words, 'I'm warning you, John. I will not allow you to push me around any longer.'"

I narrowed my eyes at the maid, and she turned a deep red and shifted her eyes down to her feet.

"Do you remember her saying that?" the chief directed to me.

I looked in my sister's big, pleading eyes, then threw my head back and winced as I said it: "Yes."

The chief's mustache drooped as he frowned.

"However," I said quickly, "how is that proof Eliza *killed* him? Spouses argue all the time, right?"

"But that wasn't all."

All eyes landed on Laura once again. What more evidence could she have? I couldn't help but want to shove a sock in her mouth to keep her from talking.

"I came back here a few minutes later because I forgot my feather duster, and I *saw* Lady Fletcher walking out of the library."

"But she had left!" I blurted out.

"I'm sorry to contradict, miss, but there was plenty of time for the lady to make her way back to her husband by the time I got there. Anyway..." She took a deep breath and continued: "Lady Fletcher left quickly without a word. I wouldn't have thought any more of it if it wasn't for the gasping and groaning coming from inside the library."

She paused, as if expecting one of us to stop her.

"And?" the chief urged.

Laura gulped. "I went in to see what the noises were all about and that's when I saw—" Her voice broke, and her shoulders shook as she was overcome by sobs.

"Ah, no need to explain what you saw next, dear. We can come to that conclusion ourselves." Chief Marsh gestured to John on the floor, and I felt sick all over again.

"Well, further investigation is needed, but this information is definitely worth looking into." The chief of police waved one of his men over to restrain Eliza. "We'll take Lady Fletcher in for questioning."

Eliza struggled against the well-built officer, but to no avail.

"I would never!" she shouted. "I loved him!"

"Wait!" Father took a few decisive steps toward her daughter and glared at the officer holding her back. Then, directed to the chief, "Surely you have had cases before where someone pretended to be someone else. I mean, look at me! I have an illusion Gift and can look like anyone I desire! Maybe someone did that."

My hands instinctively went to the necklace around my neck. I could do that, too. Of course, only with the illusion necklaces my parents made me, but what if there was someone else out there who could do something similar? With a Gift or a Melton gem? Someone really could be framing Eliza.

Chief Marsh tried to hide it, but I could still see the slight roll of his eyes. "Of course we take Mage Gifts into account, but we also have to start the investigation *somewhere*. And she has the most probable cause."

Father puffed out his chest protectively. "Then take me into custody, as well. I didn't like John, and I have an illusion Gift. Isn't that probable cause?"

"Are you admitting to the murder?"

"Of course not."

The chief muttered to himself, then nodded at

the officer restraining Eliza. The policeman released my sister, and she fell to the floor in a heap of tears.

"Fine," Chief Marsh said, "but all of you need to stick around. We'll be questioning every last one of you." He eyed each of us, including Laura.

The chief clasped his arms behind his back and circled in front of us. "I will be leaving an officer at the manor at all times while this investigation is underway. If any of you need to leave, I expect you to report to my officer, and we will have a police escort sent with you. Understood?"

I felt myself nodding, but I couldn't remember making the decision to. I wrapped my arms around myself, suddenly feeling a bitter cold as I watched the officers trail out and shut the door behind themselves. Laura followed slowly to avoid any questions from us.

Mother sank to the floor next to Eliza who was still sobbing into her hands. Father pinched the bridge of his nose and took a few deep breaths.

"There must be some mistake!" Father began pacing the room, waving his arms frustratedly.

"Are they gone?"

The sight of Uncle Morris nearly brought tears to my eyes. I wanted to hug him and beg him to fix our problem. Surely, as the head of the jail, he could talk some sense into the police.

Father tried a weak smile. "Ah, Morris. Yes, they're gone."

"Good." My uncle shoved his way past the door and tiptoed toward us, as if what he said next needed to be kept secret. "Because there's someone you should find. Someone who can help."

7

Russell

RUSSELL GAINES SAT AT HIS DINING TABLE, newspaper in one hand and a steaming cup of coffee in the other. He scowled at the first headline: "Murder at Melton Manor."

"When will all this evil come to an end?" he grumbled to himself.

But Russell felt relieved not to see his old nemesis's name splattered on the paper for once. Maybe this murder was not committed by the New Age God, and it could finally be a case that wouldn't consume Russell with guilt for not solving it.

He immediately flipped to the second page, but

he groaned as it had nothing but stories on the workers threatening to strike on their jobs, especially at the gem mines. The work was back-breaking, the conditions terrible, and the pay even worse.

It's the same thing as yesterday. When will this paper start covering something different? he thought.

Russell took a long sip of his coffee, ignoring the scalding liquid burning his tongue. It was black and bitter—absolutely perfect. And it would probably be his last cup in a while. He took another sip, savoring the taste as he swished it in his mouth before swallowing.

Scanning the newspaper before him, Russell tried to pay attention to the words he consumed. But he couldn't. He knew that within days, the money he had inherited after his father's death would run out—just as his coffee beans had this morning.

Russell set the newspaper down on top of the lace placemat. His mother had always loved setting the mats on their long dining table. He gently placed his mug right next to the paper, then rubbed the stubble on his face with his hands. The only person Russell could be angry with was himself. *He* was the one who had gambled away most of the money left to him after his father's death. And then squandered nearly the rest after his mother died shortly after.

The night before, Russell had spent the late hours and well into the morning determining what money he had left. Russell was beginning to feel sick about what he had found in his wallet. He'd even scoured the backs of dressers and underneath couch cushions. All he could come up with were just two New Age Slips he had written at the bank months ago, both worth ten full pieces. And only three quarter pieces and two crescent pieces remained in the folds of his wallet. Not enough for even just one more month maintaining his household and his debts.

It made him laugh as he had looked at the money the night before, staring at its various moon symbols and representations. He thought of Othos, the God of the Moon, upon whom Oseran money was based. If he was up there watching out for the lording families, Russell Gaines was not among the favored. And of course, if Othos *did* exist, which Russell highly doubted, the God of Beginnings would never look favorably upon someone like Russell—a gambling, cheating bastard.

His father never knew, but Russell learned as a teenager of his mother's affair with an unnamed Ufith immigrant. Yes, Russell wasn't truly the son and heir of the powerful Lord Gaines. But Russell loved his mother and never dared to reveal her secret.

"Lord Russell Gaines," he snickered at himself, scooping up and raising his mug to the empty, spacious room, "you are a fraud." He gulped his coffee down, suddenly not caring about savoring its flavor any longer.

Russell nearly dropped his favorite coffee mug as the tall doors of the dining room flew open. His butler, George Nicholson, stood tall and proud within the doorway. The tiniest hint of a smirk rested across his round, wrinkled face as he took pleasure in startling his lord.

"George. I told you to take your leave! You know I can't pay you anymore."

"You have a guest, milord," the butler said, ignoring Russell's outburst.

Russell raised a thick eyebrow. "Oh? Who on Dagirus would wish to see me?"

George moved to the side, the bright lights from the hallway reflecting on his bald head. And as he did so, a woman looking to be in her early thirties—no, forties?— strode in. But she wasn't alone. A tall police officer trailed her like a nervous dog, then positioned himself at the entrance's door frame. He was young, not someone Russell would recognize from his time working as an officer. But why would this woman have a police escort with her?

Russell sat up straight as the woman came closer. She was beautiful, with long, golden hair and delicate features that complemented the short, girlish dress she wore. Upon further observation, her confidence and maturity suggested she was at least middle-aged, but the lack of wrinkles upon her tanned skin maintained her stunning beauty.

"Are you Lord Russell Gaines?" she queried with a strong voice.

Russell nodded, lifting a cloth napkin set next to his newspaper. He dabbed at his mouth quickly, absorbing the drops of coffee at his lips before speaking.

"I am. And you are?"

She bowed her head respectfully. "Lady Melton."

Russell coughed. "*The* Lady Melton? Mother of Modernity?" Russell shot up from his chair and proffered a stiff bow. "And to what do I owe this pleasure?"

Lady Melton drew her lips into a thin line and shifted her cool eyes to the hardwood floor of the dining hall.

"Wait," Russell continued, remembering the morning's headline on the newspaper, "there was a murder at Melton Manor." Realization struck him hard, and his expression grew dark. "I don't work cases anymore, Lady Melton. Not since..." His voice trailed off, and he tightly closed his hazel eyes as thoughts of his sister flashed through his mind.

"Not since I resigned five years ago," Russell finished in a whisper.

The lady lifted her chin to meet Russell's gaze but was unable to keep her bottom lip from trembling.

"I know," she said, "I know. But—Well, this is a matter of great urgency to my family. And you were —*are*—the best!"

Russell raised a hand for her to stop, quickly losing interest. "Like I said, no more investigating. Ever."

"I can offer you money. Lots of it."

Lady Melton approached the table, her hard-soled shoes resounding loudly on the floor. She stood at the opposite end of the table from Russell, pulled from her shoulder a black leather purse, then dumped its contents onto the table. Russell's jaw dropped as he watched about fifty full pieces and five New Age Slips spill out in front of him.

"And that's just what I will pay you upfront," she said. "There will be more once you solve the crime."

Russell gulped. He swore he would never go back to crime-solving again, not after the events surrounding his sister's brutal death. But that was before he had lost nearly all of his father's fortune. He gazed at the pile of money on his table. It was enough to cover at least six months of expenses. Russell all but greedily licked his lips.

What's the harm in one more case?

"You've convinced me," he answered after a long silence.

Lady Melton gave a brilliant smile, white teeth gleaming. But Russell could have sworn he also saw a tear in her eye.

"Thank you," she said. "Thank you so much!"

~

EVEN AS AN INSPECTOR, Russell found ways to avoid the morgue. It was too bright, too clean, and smelled of way too many chemicals. It definitely was no casino.

Ah, to sit in front of a pile of poker chips and a cool glass of whiskey.

But now, he studied the body resting atop the metal table. The deceased had been tall by the looks of his gray toes peeking out from underneath the white sheet.

"Hmm..." Russell said, shoving a hand into one of his breast pockets and retrieving his flask. He unscrewed the lid quickly, then gulped its contents until the bottle was empty. It wasn't cold, but warm whiskey was better than none.

"Do you have any alcohol, Dr. Blythe?" Russell shook his empty flask in front of the mortician's face. The man moved his beady eyes from the file in front of him to Russell.

"We're not allowed to drink in here, inspector."

Russell threw a single finger in front of his face. "Not inspector. Not anymore."

He shuffled over to one of the cold room's many shelves and fumbled through the bottles.

"You sure none of these have alcohol in them?"

"Of course, I'm sure."

Russell lifted one of the heavier bottles and frowned at the word "arsenic" on the label.

"Unless you are dead yourself, none of what I have in here will be of use to you, Lord Gaines."

Russell stepped away from the chemicals and straightened his coat. "I'm not fond of 'Lord Gaines' either."

Dr. Blythe approached Russell and offered the file in his hands to him. "Then what should I call you?"

"Russell. Just call me Russell. That's my *name*, isn't it?" The former inspector studied the papers, then nodded at the body. "Marquess John Fletcher —death by stabbing. And I assume that's him?"

"Yes, yes. He was in his thirties, very healthy."

"Healthy save for the stab wound in his chest." Russell waved the file in the air. "That's what this says killed him."

The mortician raised a thin eyebrow. Shaking

his head, he slid on the pair of rubber gloves sitting on his desk, then made his way to the body. He gingerly lifted the sheet away from the deceased's torso and gestured for Russell to come closer.

"As I was saying, very healthy, save for a few scars. But the record shows the marquess was a soldier, so scars are normal." The doctor then pointed at the gaping wound in the man's chest. The cavity had since been cleaned for the autopsy, but it still looked fresh. "There's the stab wound."

Russell whistled. "Whoever killed him had to be incredibly strong. That wound is deep."

Russell circled the table. A soft glow emanated from his eyes as he activated his Mage Gift.

"And Marquess Fletcher was a large man. The stabbing from the front suggests he knew his attacker was coming. I expect he tried to put up a fight, which further suggests the killer's strength."

Dr. Blythe shrugged. "If you say so, inspe— Russell. You see things I can't." He pointed at Russell's glowing eyes. "Your Gift makes you more of an expert than I could ever be."

Russell froze and repeated the mortician's words in his mind. Maybe he would have considered himself the expert once...long ago. But not anymore. Wait, was Dr. Blythe still speaking?

"But I must concur on the deepness of the

wound. The knife had to have been pushed with great force."

"Have you found anything else on him?"

The doctor tilted his round head to the side. "Actually..."

The small man made his way over to a tray set on a separate table.

"The marquess had a lot of blood sticking a bunch of dirt and such to his clothes, but it was interesting to me that he had a fistful of this stuck to one of his palms."

The doctor guided a long set of tweezers into one of the silver trays and pulled out a handful of dark hairs.

"Those were in his palm, you say?" Russell shoved his hands behind his back and stepped closer.

The doctor nodded.

"May I take them?" Russell searched the pockets of his coat for a bag or pouch of some sort to place the hairs, but he came up empty. He felt his hands go limp. When had he *ever* come unprepared to the start of a case?

"Certainly." The doctor hurried to retrieve a paper sack. "You said that Chief Marsh ordered I help you in any way I can."

Russell gave a sheepish smile. "Yes, yes. Of *course*, he said that."

Let's just hope the chief himself doesn't learn of those particular orders.

ISSUE 15 OF 12TH MOON | THE PIRBIS NORTH DAILY

MURDER AT MELTON MANOR

Marquess John Fletcher was found dead amid the celebration of the engagement between Miss Julie Melton and Lord Calvin Sexton. All of the family, including the marquess's wife, refused to comment on the ordeal. The police say they may have a few persons of interest in mind, but Chief Marsh, head of Pirbis North Police, is not willing to divulge anything more than that (Continued on page 2).

Grow your wealth and invest in Melton gems TODAY (see page 4).

All dresses for sale at Clark's (see page 5).

The Pirbis North Daily

8

————————

Julie

"DID YOU HEAR?" A YOUNG MAN FROM OUR STAFF SAID to another servant just outside my bedroom early that morning. "Someone hired the great Inspector Gaines for this case!"

I scurried out of my warm covers and pressed my ear against the door to listen closer.

"I thought he was done solving crimes?" one of them said.

Every person in Pirbis North—actually, many throughout Osera—knew of Russell Gaines. He was the best police inspector Osera had ever seen. Russell had solved more than one hundred cases single-handedly before his twenty-fifth birthday. Half of them had been murders.

And then he abruptly left police work. At least, that's how the story went. I didn't read many newspapers or listen to local gossip, but I saw enough of the headlines while Father read *The Pirbis North Daily* at the breakfast table each morning. I knew this: Russell Gaines had spent the bulk of his career hunting down the serial killer known as the "New Age God," a nickname the criminal had coined himself. And, as far as I knew, it became too much for Inspector Gaines.

I didn't waste any time making my way back to the crime scene. I deactivated the fire gem glowing in my bedroom, then threw on the white satin robe resting at the foot of my bed. Flinging my door open, I hurried down the spiral stairs leading from the third floor to the bottom level where John's body had been found. I was *not* going to miss witnessing the legendary Inspector Gaines in action.

Servants whispered in the hall, each attempting to peek inside the library for a glance at the crime scene.

"I saw his Gift me 'self," said little Sarah, our youngest maid of only thirteen.

"No, you didn't!" said her sister Patrice, smacking Sarah at the top of her round head. "*None* of us can get a good view of what he's doing in there."

I pushed past the serving staff, ignoring their shocked whispers as I maneuvered through bare-foot and in nothing but a short robe. But I didn't care. I slid through the thin crack in the white door and entered the small library. My stomach churned as my eyes immediately went to the dried puddle of blood. They had long since taken John's body away, but I could almost see how he'd lain in a mangled heap of death.

But then I saw him.

Inspector Russell Gaines, or Lord Gaines since his retirement, was a giant. I had never seen someone that tall. I watched, incredulous, as he knelt next to the spot John's body had once been. He threw his long, black overcoat back behind himself and rubbed a thoughtful hand over the shadow of beard growing along his angular jaw. His black fedora tipped forward ever so slightly, revealing the thick golden-brown hair that reached a little past his ears.

I tiptoed closer to look at the inspector using the Mage Gift that had become so famous.

"Stay back, miss," Chief Marsh instructed me. He sat in the little armchair in the corner as Lord Gaines worked. The chief's stubby arms crossed tightly over his bulging belly. I hadn't even noticed him there.

"Oh, Julie. You didn't bother to dress?" Mother's soft voice startled me, as well.

I whirled around to see my parents standing next to the door, tapping their feet and wringing their hands as the inspector circled the room continuously.

"Oh, no matter, Lady Melton," the inspector chimed in. "She doesn't do it for me."

My face grew warm at his horrible remark. I opened my mouth to snap at him, but Inspector Gaines hadn't taken his eyes away from the crime scene even once to look in my direction.

I shook my head, trying to ignore his impoliteness, and stood next to my parents. But my eyes never left the inspector. I gasped as I finally saw it: The shadows of his tan face were illuminated from the dull, yellow glow of his large eyes. Legend said Russell Gaines could detect the smallest clues and deduce the most challenging problems with the help of his Mage Gift, and his glowing eyes were an indication that he was using it.

A shiver went down my spine as a thought entered my mind: What if he could see my secrets with just a single look at me? I clutched my chest and urged myself to continue breathing. I shouldn't worry about that—he wasn't investigating me; he was investigating a murder that I had nothing to do with.

I looked again at the inspector's glowing eyes. What was he staring at?

I craned my neck forward, trying to see what caught the inspector's stare. He shoved a hand in one of his coat's deep pockets as he gazed at the blood on the wooden floor next to where John's head had been.

"Well?" Chief Marsh demanded gruffly. "Have you seen anything worth looking into, inspector?"

Lord Gaines cleared his throat, but his glowing eyes continued to scan the body before him. "Marsh, I am not an inspector anymore. Don't call me that."

I snickered as Marsh's cherub face went red.

"Have you seen anything?" the chief said through gritted teeth.

"I have seen lots of things." Lord Gaines's voice was smooth and calm. I couldn't help but admire the way the man held himself.

But just as those words fell from his mouth, his eyes dulled. The inspector turned quickly on the heel of his boot, swiftly marched out of the library, and turned a corner, away from the chattering serving staff.

"Uh..." Father said.

Chief Marsh groaned and palmed his forehead.

"He's always doing this type of thing. Stay where you are. He'll be back."

And back he was. Just a few seconds passed before Russell shoved the door open and strode back into the room. Inspector—or Lord Gaines—or Russell—whatever he wanted us to call him—took his place standing before us. He adjusted the hat atop his head, then clasped his gloved hands behind his back.

"I will say this once," he said, "and only once, so all of you must listen carefully." Then, without turning around to face where the chief sat, he said, "That includes you, Marsh."

We all remained silent, eyes glued on the famous inspector before us. Even Marsh didn't complain and sat on the edge of his seat.

"As I said, I have seen many things, but I will mention just two clues." He waved two fingers in front of us with narrowed eyes. "Only two because the others are only relevant for me to know at this moment."

"But we're paying you to be here," Father said with narrowed eyes.

Russell waved his words away.

"What about me? Don't you trust me?" Chief Marsh whined.

"Quiet, Marsh. It has nothing to do with trust and everything to do with intelligence."

The chief's nostrils flared as he muttered obscenities under his breath.

Russell pointed a single finger in the air.

"First," he continued, "we must consider the contents enclosed in the victim's fist." Russell pulled a paper sack from inside his coat, then dumped its contents into his palm. He showed us a handful of dark hairs. "These hairs indicate a struggle. And two—"

"In the victim's fist?" I interjected.

He raised an eyebrow at me. "Yes, these were in his fist."

"And how did you come by these hairs?" Marsh queried with a growing scowl on his face.

"Oh, I stopped by the morgue first. Can't solve a murder without seeing the body." He glanced at each of us while tapping his foot impatiently. "May I continue?"

There was hesitation, but soon we nodded in response. Chief Marsh, however, grumbled something about Russell and the morgue.

The former inspector gave us a hint of an excited smile. "And second, the victim wrote a message on the floor in his own blood."

My family and I were too stunned to reply, but Chief Marsh leaped from his seat and approached Russell.

"What?" Marsh cried, getting on his hands and

knees to study the floor, stained red from John's blood. "Where did you see that?"

Russell bent over and gave a sharp blow to the top of the chief's head. I jumped, shocked.

"Well, you played the usual idiot and moved his body before inspecting the surroundings, Marsh. You must have smeared the message and failed to notice. See here." Russell pointed at a section of the blood on the floor.

We all inched forward a little closer. And then I saw what he meant—at least, I *thought* I did. Whereas the rest of the blood had pooled around the body in a puddle, the blood Russell pointed to displayed a bloodied pattern of various, unnatural scribbles. Cocking my head to the side, I deciphered what looked to be an "N" followed by an "O," a "T," "E," and then an "L." The rest of the message had been much too ruined to decipher.

"But what does it say?" I blurted out.

Russell raised an interested brow in my direction, taking in my inappropriate attire with a smirk.

"Well, there are many possibilities as to what the marquess's last words could have been. But I took the liberty to come up with the answer."

"Is that what you were doing when you left?" the chief snapped. He stood once again and shoved a finger in Russell's face.

Grinning, Russell pulled a thin notebook from

an inside pocket and brandished it for all of us to see.

"Of course. It took me longer than I wanted, but..." He trailed off, opening the leather notebook and flipping through the pages.

I scoffed. *It only took him a few seconds.*

"Ah," he said, "here it is. Considering the other clues and who the police's main suspect is, I was able to determine that his message most likely reads, 'Not Eliza.'"

The silence was agonizing. Not even Chief Marsh had a reply for Lord Gaines's revelation.

Finally, Father spoke up: "It wasn't Eliza?" The hope etched onto his face lit up his strong features. "But how did your clues bring you to that conclusion? You just found hair in John's fist."

Russell shook his head. "Time will tell if I'm correct."

Father raised a dark brow as the man hadn't answered his question, but he retreated and folded his arms. After all, Inspector Gaines was famous for his ability to solve near-impossible cases—all thanks to his Mage Gift.

Mother laughed jubilantly. "I knew Eliza didn't do it!"

I couldn't contain my joy, either. I smiled along with my mother and released a relieved sigh.

"However..."

We all ceased celebrating and looked to Russell. He tapped his chin thoughtfully.

"It *could* still be Lady Fletcher, though I highly doubt it. But I have two suspects that are more likely to have killed the marquess than she." He eyed the three of us with a twinkle in his eye. Was he enjoying this?

He looked at Father and me. "Your Mage Gifts are quite famous in Pirbis North," Russell said, focusing on Father. "Your illusion Gift is quite remarkable, and yours..." He turned his eyes to me. They were glowing slightly, and I shivered. "Yours is notable, as well."

I gulped and met eyes with my father, who furrowed his dark brows as he scowled.

"What are you implying?" Father demanded.

Russell pulled a silver flask from another hidden pocket and took a swig of its contents. He sighed happily as he swallowed, taking his time to screw the lid back on and replace it in its hiding place.

"Thanks for the whiskey, by the way, Lady Melton. I was in desperate need of a refill."

I clenched and unclenched my fists. "Sir, you were saying?"

Russell flashed a look at me, his eyes glowing once again. I squirmed uncomfortably, shrinking underneath his stare. But he didn't study my face—

his eerie eyes remained on my head of chestnut hair. His eyes then moved to my father's matching dark hair, but for what purpose?

"Since the both of you could easily place upon yourselves an illusion of Lady Fletcher, and both of you could potentially have a good motive, it is quite possible the killer is either Lord Melton or Miss Julie Melton."

9

Julie

WHAT HAPPENED NEXT WAS A BLUR. I VAGUELY HEARD
Father arguing with Russell Gaines. The former
inspector indifferently listened to the lord's shouts,
and Mother wrapped me in her arms protectively.

Father or I killed John? My thoughts churned
violently, and I felt as if I would be sick. I knew I
didn't do it, but Father...

Chief Marsh rubbed his face, looking exasperated. "We've already thought of the possibility of
Lord Melton, Gaines. *Of course*, we have. The
thought of the younger Miss Melton crossed my
mind, too. But there were so many other people

here that night. There might be a dozen other Gifts that could have aided in making the killer look like Eliza. And half of those might even be people with dark brown hair."

"Yes, yes, Marsh. I know all this," Russell snapped. "I only said it's more possible for those two to have done it than Eliza Fletcher. I didn't say anything about not wanting to investigate everyone else."

Eyes wide, I looked over to Father. He was fuming. I had never seen him so vocal or angry than what I had witnessed in the last few hours. But he would *never*. Would he? He never particularly liked John Fletcher, especially once the man had started mistreating Eliza.

My heart stopped as I remembered John's last words to my sister: "I am so tired of your father meddling in our affairs!" Had they been arguing about him?

"And what about Lady Melton?" Chief Marsh added. "She can copy any Gift and use it herself in any object. Couldn't she have done it?"

Russell barked out a laugh. "Of course not. Look at the hairs. They belong to someone with darker-colored hair. Lady Melton has the most yellow hair I have ever seen. Also, she hired me. Now, either she's a cocky killer who thinks she's too clever to get caught, or she wants the true culprit found."

"Lord Melton," Russell continued, "will you put an illusion of Lady Fletcher on yourself?"

Father's face shook with rage. "You think I did it?"

"If you please, I'd like to see your Gift."

"I wasn't fond of John Fletcher, but I would *never* take someone's life!" Father cried.

Russell didn't flinch at Father's outburst.

Father ran a hand through his hair with a sigh. Then, as he closed his eyes, a flash of color danced downward from his head until he didn't look like himself anymore. He was Eliza. Even his clothes appeared as a simple evening gown. I knew, though, from personal experience, that if I reached over to touch the golden locks and soft face, I would feel Father's features on my fingers.

Russell nodded thoughtfully. "Yes, very convincing. Now you."

It took me a moment to realize Russell was looking at me. I blinked rapidly as I tried to process his words.

"What?" I squeaked.

"Please place an illusion of your sister on yourself."

I gulped. I didn't have the right necklace! Did he know that? Was he toying with me?

"I—I can't! I have to prepare. I have to—"

"Oh, uh, Julie's Gift doesn't work quite like

mine," Father stammered. He looked in my direction, and I could see in his eyes that he would try his best to help keep my truth a secret.

Russell held up a hand. "Never mind. I've seen enough for now."

I wanted to back into a corner and hide.

What did he mean, "I've seen enough for now"? I thought. *He knows. He* has *to know.*

Chief Marsh shook his head. "Well, if the two of you are our most likely suspects... Lord Melton, Miss Julie, I am going to take you into custody for the time being."

Chief Marsh moved to restrain me and called for another officer to take Father, but Russell raised a hand to stop him.

"That's not how I do things," he said. "I need to see what my suspects do on a daily basis. In fact, is Eliza Fletcher in custody?"

The chief rolled his eyes and stepped away from me. "No, but she has been placed in her room and under careful watch."

"Let her roam about as she pleases. I'd like to observe her, as well."

Chief Marsh's jaw dropped. "B...but, Inspector—"

Lord Gaines rubbed his face, exasperated. "Stop calling me that."

Marsh threw his head back and sighed. "Lord Gaines—"

"Just Russell will do."

"Russell," the Chief hissed through gritted teeth, "if one of them truly is the murderer, we can't have them running off, can we?"

Russell shrugged. "We'll just have to assign officers to keep an eye on them. I'll take charge of Miss Julie. She intrigues me."

He eyed me with a hint of a glow to his eyes, and suddenly, anger replaced my anxiety. I glared at Lord Gaines, arms stiff and head hurting as I turned and stormed out of the library.

~

I RUMMAGED through the drawers and cabinets in my bedroom, searching for the necklace.

"Where is it?" I whimpered. "It *has* to be here!"

I moved over to my large vanity, sat at the plush chair before it, and pulled my jewelry box in front of me. I'd already gone through its contents a dozen times, but I was so anxious that I felt the need to go through it once again. I pulled open the golden latch and lifted the lid. The top drawer of the box contained all of the earrings I never bothered to wear. I removed the top container to reveal the necklaces underneath.

I tore through the chains, untangling them as I went. My eyes desperately searched for the right one.

And then I saw it.

With a relieved sigh, I pulled the thin gold chain from the bottom of the box and smiled as the little red stone at its center glinted from the light coming from the glass lamp beside my mirror.

"Well, that answers that question," I said aloud. "No one stole the necklace to look like Eliza."

I slowly set the chain back into the box. Leaving the jewelry box open, I moved to my bed. I landed on my back with a groan, my body bouncing three times on the springy mattress before it stopped.

Almost immediately after I stormed away from the crime scene, the thought entered my mind that somebody who knew of my secret would steal the necklace I used to create an illusion of my sister. But that didn't seem to be the case. I felt both relieved and saddened.

Relieved because no unwanted person knew my secret but saddened because one of the scenarios that would have exonerated my father and Eliza wasn't viable. Father had his own Gift to look like Eliza, and Eliza didn't need to change herself.

"You weren't supposed to run off, Miss Melton."

I shot straight up in my bed, turned my head to the new voice, then scowled once I saw who it was.

"Inspector Gaines," I grumbled. Then, realizing I was still in nothing but a robe, I pulled the smooth cloth tightly over my chest. "This is my personal room."

Russell traipsed about the length of the room. He glanced quickly at my jewelry box and snickered to himself. My heart began to pound. Had he watched me search through it? How long had he been standing there in my room, just observing?

He then raised an eyebrow at the bright white rug and the equally white wallpaper.

"Just call me Russell," he said. "I'm not an inspector anymore. And what's with all the white? Don't you know *off*-white is all the rage these days?"

My scowl deepened as I slid myself off the mattress to face him. "*Russell*," I spat. "If you wouldn't mind, I'd like to get dressed."

He scowled. "Ugh, fine. But be quick about it."

"*Alone.*"

"I can turn around."

After many seconds without an answer from me, he sighed and shoved his hands in his coat pockets.

"Very well," he replied. "But I am standing outside. I am in charge of your whereabouts for the next while, you know."

He gave me another one of his glowing stares. I froze underneath, sure his eyes were searching through my mind. But he didn't say a word as he dimmed the glow and exited, clicking the door shut.

I released a long, shaky breath, then stepped over to my dresser next to the small hearth in my bedroom. I pulled open the top drawer and made a triumphant grunt as I grabbed the simple shirt and pants folded neatly in the corner. The party was over, and I wasn't about to wear another dress for a long time.

I sighed happily once I was dressed—not just for the comfort the outfit brought me but also for the pocketed pants that allowed me to keep more than a few illusion necklaces. Who knew what situations might present themselves now with the need for an illusion—or *many* illusions?

Searching through my pants' pockets, I found the black satin ribbon I always kept handy and tied my thick hair into a tail. As I did so, I strode back to my jewelry box. I studied the many necklaces at its base, placed one golden chain with a pearl pendant topped with the tiniest diamond into a hidden pocket within my shirt, and shoved a couple of other necklaces in each visible trousers pocket, then another few in the hidden one within my right pant leg. I couldn't help but snicker at the one similarity between Russell and me: we both seemed to have a multitude of pockets—possibly for different reasons, but it was an interesting fact.

I placed the earring drawer at the top of my jewelry box, slid the case back into place on my vanity, then pulled on my boots. Taking a deep breath, I turned the brass knob of my bedroom door and saw Russell standing directly in front of it with a big, goofy grin on his face.

"Interesting apparel," he said as he tapped his chin. "I think I prefer the robe."

I rolled my eyes and stepped over the threshold, using every ounce of restraint not to smack the man over his head. Russell Gaines was *not* turning out how I'd imagined him.

The romantic part of myself had imagined the man, only six years my senior, might make me swoon. Of course, even in my imaginings, it never went further than that. But seeing him and his rude personality in person, I wasn't even *close* to adoring the man. Sure, he was handsome, and his detecting and solving skills were of legend, but so far, I couldn't stand him.

But I couldn't help but wonder if he'd always been like that. Was there something that happened in his past to make him bitter at the world and everything in it?

"Come," Russell said, marching toward the spiral staircase, "we have a lot of work to do."

"*We?*"

"Of course. If you're not the killer, maybe you'll be of use to me in other ways. We'll see."

Russell skipped down each step. I followed slowly, hand on the banister, and studied the back of his head.

Why did he take this case after being retired for so long? I wondered.

Once we reached the bottom of the spiral staircase, Russell whirled around to me with a dramatic *swoosh* of his coat.

"Chief Marsh informed me that the time of death was about an hour and a half into the party. Where were you at that time?"

Russell wasn't looking at me, but I could clearly see the dull glow of his eyes shining from behind his bangs.

I scoffed. "I was at the par—" I stopped. No, I wasn't at the party. At that particular time, I was still strolling the halls by myself on the way back to the ballroom. I didn't have an alibi!

Russell cleared his throat. "Yes?"

"I was by myself," I said in hushed tones. "I saw Eliza arguing with John, and then I made my way back to the party. Well, I also saw the maid Laura for a bit, but I left quickly after."

Russell nodded and didn't say another word as we walked side by side. I couldn't stop my hands from shaking as I wiped the drops of sweat falling into my brow.

"And for how long were you planning on killing your brother-in-law?"

His words made me stop midstep. My jaw went slack, and my heart dropped to my stomach.

"What?"

"You heard me." Russell had stopped as well, but he still wasn't looking in my direction.

"I didn't. I never. I wouldn't kill someone!"

"Interesting," he said, resuming our stroll.

I rubbed my face with my hands and bit back my tears. *Does he really think I'm the killer? Or is he just playing with my emotions to see how I'll react?*

"Julie!"

A smile immediately snapped onto my face at the sound of Calvin's kind voice. I hadn't seen him since the night before. I'd almost forgotten he and his mother would still be at the manor.

I could almost hear Mother's voice in my head as if she would say, "They're already family! They should stay with us in our home. A murder shouldn't tear us apart."

"Calvin!" I cried, rushing to him.

Without thinking, I threw my arms around Calvin's neck. He stumbled slightly underneath my weight but quickly wrapped his own arms around my waist. Face growing warm, I realized what I had just done and retreated from Calvin's grip.

"Sorry," I muttered, "it's been a long few hours, and I was just happy to see you."

Calvin flashed me a brilliant, crooked smile and fondly brushed a finger across my nose.

"It was nice," he said.

"And who might this be?" Russell stood directly behind us with an amused look on his face.

"Uh, this is Lord Calvin Sexton. My fiancé."

"Ah." Russell approached Calvin and outstretched a gloved hand.

Calvin hesitated but then shook the former inspector's hand slowly. "Are you Inspector Gaines? *The* great Inspector Russell Gaines?"

"That's me. Former inspector, but still great. "

Calvin's face lit up like a little boy gifted the toy he wanted all year.

"You're joking! That's incredible!" Calvin continued to clutch Russell's hand, too excited to remember to let go.

"Uh, yes. Quite incredible." Russell pulled his hand away from Calvin's grip and shook the feeling back into his fingers. "You're rather strong, aren't you, Lord Sexton?"

Calvin chuckled. "So sorry! I've just read all about your cases. I've been a fan for years."

"Yes, well, I don't solve crime anymore. Just

doing a favor for the Melton family." Russell gave a short nod, then began walking back in the direction we had initially been heading.

"Come, Miss Melton!" he called to me without a pause in his steps.

"Well, he's friendly." Calvin laughed.

I snorted. "You have no idea."

"Come!"

Calvin raised an eyebrow as Russell called for me once again. "Why must you go with him?"

My smile quickly turned to a frown, and I dropped my gaze to the floor. I didn't quite know how to answer his question. Russell *had* said something about being intrigued by me. Why? I prayed to Othos it had nothing to do with my lack of Gift. All I *did* know was that I was a suspect. How would Calvin react if he knew I was suspected for the murder? Would that scare him? Would he not want anything to do with me?

"I'm just helping him with the case, is all. Mother hired him, and I wanted to make sure it wasn't in vain."

As I said it, I realized I *did* want to help with the case. I wanted to make sure this killer was found. Even if I had to stay at the right hand of a man who could learn my secrets with just a look. But why hadn't he found out I didn't have a Gift yet? Especially if his eyes could do what legend said they could? Could he only see clues to things he was currently solving?

Calvin rested a hand on my shoulder comfortingly, but his face grew solemn. He seemed to notice my concern and forced a smile.

"I understand. Just don't go falling for the great Inspector Gaines. Meet me for dinner, maybe?"

I glanced up at the ceiling so Calvin might avoid seeing the tears well up in my eyes. I didn't know how long I was to be a suspect in this horrible crime, and the inspector wasn't very keen on leaving me alone.

"I'll try my best," I said.

Russell threw his body around the corner he had just turned and waved me on, exasperated.

"Sorry, I must go."

I moved to run off after Russell, but Calvin grabbed my hand and kissed it. My stomach did flips at his touch. Then, with a gentle nod of his head, Calvin left the way he had come.

I finally caught up to Russell. Once I reached his side, he tilted his hat forward, obscuring his face in shadow, and ambled on even faster.

"Hey," I shouted, increasing my speed, "wait up! Where are we going, anyway?"

"To question a few people. This is where the investigation *really* begins."

10

Julie

"I don't see why this is necessary," Russell said, glaring at the officer sticking small gems attached to wires to Laura's forehead.

"What does it do?" I breathed incredulously.

Chief Marsh patted the box resting on the short dining table in the servants' wing. The wires from Laura's head were connected to it. "It will tell us if she's lying. We'll probably be using it on you too, miss."

I gulped. A machine to detect if I was lying? What if they asked me about my Gift? If Russell didn't find out the truth about me, surely this machine would! I'd heard rumors about the truth gems, but it was one of the few inventions that didn't come from Mother.

"Like I said," Russell growled, "this is not necessary. I never needed one of these when I was an inspector."

"The truth gems didn't exist when you worked for us."

"Exactly. They didn't exist because *I* was there. Who needs a fancy machine when you have me?" For added effect, Russell brought a bright glow to his eyes. Laura looked awestruck, her own eyes widening.

"How does it work?" I whispered.

Chief Marsh pointed at the red gems attached to Laura's head. "They'll glow if she's lying to us. A few force gems inside the box send power through the wires, and the gems on her head will detect increases in pulse. And if your pulse quickens, that usually means you're lying."

Laura didn't seem the least bit nervous. She just gazed at Russell with a hand clutched to her heart. But I was feeling increasingly warm. I wiped a shaky finger over the sweat forming on my forehead.

"Alright, you can start now, Gaines." Chief Marsh found a seat in the back of the room. The officer who placed the wires on Laura's head took his place by the truth gems box.

Russell rolled his eyes but then gave a kind smile to Laura. "Can you explain, in detail, who you saw the night of the marquess's death?"

Her eyes grew wide, and she grabbed at her seat like it would save her from her memories. "It was awful. I saw—I saw *her.*"

I flinched at the words coming from Laura's mouth. I knew she spoke of my sister. But Laura didn't seem comfortable, either. Before, her nerves didn't seem to have ailed her. But now, she shifted on her stool and crossed and uncrossed her legs over and over again. The fresh linens she had behind her stopped folding themselves as she lost focus on using her Mage Gift to levitate and control them.

"Who exactly?" Russell leaned forward. His eyes burned a dim yellow.

"Lady Eliza Fletcher." She gulped as she glanced in my direction. "She walked straight out the library door with a... You know, it was quite the mischievous grin—the most mischievous and *evil* a grin I ever saw."

"And what did you do next?"

Laura wiped her palms along on her brown uniform skirt. "Uh, I saw blood on her clothes, and I heard a lot of gasping and moaning in the library, Inspector."

"He's not an inspector anymore, Lau—"

"Of course, I am," Russell said, interrupting me and winking at the maid. The woman, who had a good few years on Russell, flushed a deep red and giggled.

I rolled my eyes. "So? You were worried?"

She nodded. "Yes, I went inside, and I..." Laura's bottom lip trembled, and she clutched her chest with both of her hands.

Russell inched himself to the edge of his seat and placed comforting hands on the maid's knees. "It's alright. We know what you saw."

My initial reaction was to gag at his flirtation, but upon further observation, I could see his genuine empathy by the drawing in of his thick brows and the pursing of his lips. Only Othos knew what horrible things the man had seen as an inspector.

"Is there anything else?" The maid queried, eyes continuously glancing at Russell's hands on her knee.

He snapped back up and clapped his hands together. "That is all for now. Don't worry; we'll let you know if we need you again."

"Wait!" I said. "Can I ask something?"

Russell stretched back with a loud yawn, but he didn't say no.

I looked toward Laura. She avoided my eyes. I didn't blame her for feeling uneasy with me; I felt the same toward her.

"You told us yesterday that you heard my sister and her husband arguing, but I didn't see you. Why were you there?"

She shrugged. "Maids are always cleaning the halls at the manor, right? I was just around the corner, and you were too distracted to see me, I guess."

I glanced at the truth gems on her forehead, but they remained their dull, red color. No sign of any glowing to indicate her lying.

I shivered to feel a pair of eyes boring into me, then nearly jumped out of my seat to see Russell staring at me with mouth agape.

"What?" I demanded.

"I can't believe I didn't think to ask that." Russell rubbed a hand along his leg, eyebrows furrowing and frown growing on his face. He seemed disturbed.

"Again, thank you for your time." Russell leaped up, suddenly in brighter spirits, and strode out of the room. Sighing, I tried a smile at Laura. She gave a small one in return.

"Russell, wait!" I cried, jumping out of my seat

and sprinting over the threshold leading out of the servants' wing.

And then I saw Eliza.

Russell stopped, too, finger tapping his chin as my frazzled sister scurried through the halls toward the kitchens, flanked by two police officers. Eliza's pretty satin party dress was wrinkled, her hair was ratted, and her eyes were sunken and black. She walked quickly, as if she didn't want to be seen by anyone.

"I'm just getting some lunch," she muttered to the policemen. "There's no need for the two of you to follow me everywhere I go."

"Eliza!" I called, waving my arm and swallowing back the lump in my throat that threatened tears. I'd almost forgotten she'd been here all along, holed up in her room.

Eliza's tightly folded arms and lack of eye contact answered my previous question: She didn't want to see anyone—even me.

The group reached close enough that I could touch her. I moved to do so but retracted as Eliza gave me a bloodshot look.

With a hoarse whisper, she said, "Please, Julie, leave me alone."

11

Julie

FATHER WAS NOT HAPPY ABOUT THE TALL, BRUTISH-looking policeman standing guard over him as he worked in his study. The officer stood firm and at attention in the far corner of the office, eyeing Father, who sat at his desk with narrowed eyes. My father rested his face in his hands as he muttered quietly to himself.

"Lord Melton!" Russell traipsed into the study and gave a quick bow. "How has your morning been?"

Father chuckled, the sound muffled by his hands. And then there was silence.

Russell looked at me with his brows drawn together in mock seriousness. "Is he normally this quiet?"

Before I could answer, Father let out a loud groan and planted his ocean-blue eyes on Russell.

"It has not been the best morning, Inspector." Father glared at Russell. "Did you think it would be going *well*?"

Russell ignored his question and threw himself into the chair in front of Father's desk, his long coat flying as he did so.

"Do I need to send out a memo? Just call me Russell. No 'Inspector,' no 'Lord,' just...*Russell*." He said his name slowly while pointing at his lips as if teaching a child how to speak.

Father's face turned red for a moment, but then he just looked away and placed his hands on his lap.

"What can I do for you, Russell?" he said.

"Actually, it's what you can do for your daughter." Russell waved me over as he leaned back and balanced on just two legs of the chair.

"What? I don't—Do you not have investigative questions for my father?"

Russell shrugged and once again pulled out his flask of alcohol. I licked my lips, suddenly craving a bit of spirit to calm myself.

"I don't know. I thought you could ask him some questions first," Russell said between swigs.

I gaped at him. Was this part of his process? I swallowed loudly and tried a smile at Father. He smiled back, but only for a split second before the worry lines in his forehead returned.

I racked my brain as to what Russell would want me to ask. So, I started with the most obvious question:

"Father..." I paused, choking back the lump that suddenly appeared in my throat. "Did you do it?"

Father looked to me, eyelids growing stiff as tears filled his eyes. "Of course not, Julie," he said calmly.

"Where were you at the time of his death?" Russell countered.

Father threw his head back and let out a short sigh. "I was in here. My office. Right after I ate and the dancing started, I went to—"

His voice broke, and my face fell as my father began to sob.

"Please," I said. "We shouldn't torture him."

Russell held up a finger, placed the chair back in its usual position on all four legs, and leaned over the desk.

"Finish what you were saying, Lord Melton."

Father rubbed his chin as if to force himself back into reality before speaking. "Before the party,

I had a disagreement with John about finances and what I was planning on doing with the Melton fortune. You see, since he had married my eldest daughter, he became my marquess. He and Eliza were to inherit all the money and the manor, but..." He trailed off, ashamedly glancing in my direction.

"It's alright," I whispered.

Father nodded and continued: "I told him I didn't want to leave him the money anymore. He grew furious at me, demanding a reason, and I said something about his anger and temper toward my daughter. And then he left, raving something about making Eliza use her Mage Gift to make them more money than I would ever have in my possession."

"I assume you didn't like John for mistreating your daughter," Russell said, tapping his chin.

Father twiddled his thumbs absent-mindedly. "I really didn't."

"That does establish some motive, but that does not tell me where you were when he was killed, my lord."

Father bowed his head. "I left to work in here. I was going through the books to see what I could do to help John and Eliza without giving them everything after my death. Especially Eliza. It's not fair to her. But I swear to Othos, I didn't kill him."

"Interesting," Russell said, his eyes suddenly glowing.

"Gaines!"

I jumped at the sound of Chief Marsh's gruff voice. The man stormed into the room and stopped, hands planted firmly on his hips. An officer trailed behind, holding the truth gem machine.

"You can't just run off like that! We wanted to hook up the truth gems to Lord Melton while you questioned him."

"And that's exactly why I ran off. Those are a waste of time." Russell waved a dismissive hand in the machine's direction. "And I can do whatever I want, Marsh. I don't work for you. At the moment, I work for the Meltons." Then, directed to my father, Russell said, "Would you like me to hook you up to the truth gems?"

"Uh, only if you think they'll tell you something," Father replied.

The chief's mouth fell open, and he looked as if he wanted to bite Russell's head off, but he merely shook his head.

"Fine, but once you are finished, Gaines, we will do our own questioning."

"Oh, I'm finished." Russell nodded thoughtfully as he stood. He shook Father's hand. "Thank you for your time, Lord Melton."

∽

WE WERE WALKING AGAIN—AIMLESSLY, it seemed. Russell whistled an unfamiliar tune, and I grew more nervous by the second.

"What next?" I dared to say.

Russell stopped whistling and licked his lips. "We are going to look at the list of all the party guests and staff present during the murder. Then, we'll study the coinciding registries from their areas to determine what Mage Gift each person has."

I groaned, dreading how boring something like that sounded, but then I thought of something: "Does that mean you have moved on from Father, Eliza, and me as suspects?"

If my family was no longer under scrutinization, maybe this madness could come to an end, and I could go back to hiding my secrets away from the world.

"Of course not," Russell scoffed. "But only a terrible inspector would too soon let go of the possibility of more than just a couple suspects. We must turn every stone."

I sighed. It would have been too easy, anyway. I went right back to feeling sick to my stomach.

"Russell, why did you have me ask my father that question?"

He halted and turned to me with the hint of a smile. "First of all, I didn't tell you to ask him if he killed your brother-in-law. But, I hoped you would. I wanted to see his reaction when you asked if he killed the marquess. I learned a lot from it."

Russell continued his walk and started to whistle once again.

I clenched my fists and glared at the man. "And? What did you determine?"

Russell only continued to walk and whistle, ignoring my question. I threw my hands up in exasperation. I had no choice but to follow him.

12

Julie

THE REGISTRIES WERE EXTENSIVE. I YAWNED AS I pulled the fifth list from the large stack Russell and I were poring over.

"Are they all there?" Chief Marsh grumbled.

Russell had requested we conduct our search in the grand ballroom. We sat in the center of the cool, marble floor. The glass chandelier above us dangled brightly; Russell had demanded its lighting. The nearly one hundred light gems struck me as perhaps *too* bright to study the papers.

"I believe so," Russell answered, nose deep in

several files at once. "Don't worry; I will call for you if there is an issue."

The chief turned away, slamming the double doors behind him, the sound echoing loudly through the empty room. The decorations and tables had been taken down hours prior.

"Does he not like you?" I asked, setting down a registry. I rubbed my temples; my head pounded.

Russell shrugged, not moving his glowing eyes away from his papers even once. "I guess not. We always argued when I was on the force, but he appreciated my results." He glanced at me for a split second, and I shivered as I met his glowing gaze. "And I *always* brought results."

His last few words almost sounded like a threat —for my sake. My lip trembled slightly as I picked up the list again.

Oseran law required recording of all Mage Gifts of every citizen. The lists helped government officials and the police in keeping track of the people. And, in cases like ours, only Oserans with specific bestowed Gifts could commit certain crimes—such as someone turning into Eliza to kill John. Best to keep track of everyone's potential criminal abilities.

Each lording family was in charge of keeping a record of the area they presided over. So, the records Father kept and turned in regularly to the government and Pirbis North police were among our stack. Russell had asked for copies of all corresponding registries for every guest. It had taken Marsh and his men nearly five hours to procure it all.

"I still don't completely understand what I'm looking for."

Russell shook his head. "Look for any names of the party guests who match the registries, and then let me know if you see a Mage Gift that could have assisted in your brother-in-law's murder. You know, something like that."

I rubbed my eyes before taking another glance at the copy of the guest list Mother had provided for us, then the corresponding registries for each name. I scanned over a dozen Gifts. The Gifts varied greatly—from reading minds to seeing in the dark, and even one person who could speak with rats.

But it was difficult to keep my mind from wandering. After all, reading through a list of primarily meaningless names was rather dull. My thoughts drifted to more pressing issues, such as Russell's suspicion of my family, or a murderer running loose. But mostly, I thought of the former inspector sitting just a few feet away from me. Part of me wanted to ask him why I intrigued him so, and the other part of me just wanted to keep quiet and hope he kept me around merely to rule me out as a suspect.

I tried to think of something else, but then the image of John's lifeless, bloodied body kept flashing through my mind.

I set the paper on my knees and held my breath against the flipping and churning of my stomach. The only dead person I'd seen besides John's was my grandmother at her funeral. And she looked peaceful, her arms folded neatly across her chest and a hint of a smile on her painted lips. But she *died* peacefully. John, obviously, did not.

Muffled shouting from outside the ballroom granted me a welcome release from my thoughts. The doors swung open, letting in a *whoosh* of cool air, and through them came Marsh. His chubby hand had turned white as it gripped the strong arm of Calvin as the chief pulled the young man in the room with him.

"I saw him lurking near the ballroom here, Gaines."

Marsh shoved Calvin forward, making him stumble before he caught his balance and straightened a stray, chestnut hair across his forehead in embarrassment.

The chief of police pursed his lips at Calvin and shook his head. "Probably tryin' to spy and such, I think."

Without a glance away from the papers he studied, Russell chuckled. "*Or* he wished to remain near his fiancée."

Calvin looked in my direction and flashed me a charming smile, his embarrassment dissipating as he did so.

"I'm hoping I can take Miss Melton out for dinner tonight."

Calvin clasped his hands behind his back and winked at me. My heart skipped a beat, and I bit my lip as I shifted my gaze to my knees.

"Go right ahead," Russell said as he pulled a list closer to his glowing eyes.

My mouth fell open, and I inched my body forward in anticipation. "Really?"

Before Russell could reply, Marsh cleared his throat. "What? But she's a *suspect*! You're gonna let her off on her own while an investigation is in progress?"

Sighing, Russell pinched the bridge of his nose and set his stack of papers down. "Fine. Send them with one of your officers." He directed his attention to Calvin. "And tell me where you're taking her and for how long."

Calvin nodded. "Of course. Makes perfect sense."

My shoulders hunched forward in relief as some of the tension in my body released. Taking a break from the chaos—even for a short time—would be wonderful. And I couldn't help but feel excited to spend more time with Calvin. I had hoped this weekend would provide the two of us more opportunity to acquaint ourselves with one another...maybe even spark something more romantic between us.

I looked up at my fiancé. With an even larger smile than before, he took a few steps closer and offered a hand to help me from the floor.

"Shall we, milady?"

I took his hand, ignoring the glares from Chief Marsh, and smiled back. "We shall."

~

I SCRATCHED at the fishnet stockings that were hugging my legs a little too tightly, then pulled at the short hemline of the black dress I'd thrown on before leaving with Calvin for dinner. He took me to the city—to a nice restaurant. One with mahogany tables, gold-rimmed wine glasses, and chains of diamonds hanging from every woman's neck. Most people would wear fake jewelry or pearls, knowing the high demand for gems to be used in our country's machines, but these people seemed too rich to care.

I pulled up a strap of my dress that had slipped off my shoulder. I knew my mother would drop dead if I'd gone on a date in pants rather than a nice dress, so I chose to forgo my comfort. But I still regretted the wardrobe choice every time a draft of air blew up my legs. Dresses were so inconvenient. At least this one had a few hidden pockets for my necklaces.

"Julie? Are you alright?"

I jumped a bit as Calvin's words roused me from my trance.

"Oh," I replied, straightening my shoulders against the wooden back of my seat, "yes, sorry. What was it you said?"

Calvin chuckled and dabbed at his mouth with a napkin, then set it back next to his glass plate piled with steaming pork and greens.

"I inquired after your childhood. I know it's a general question, but I think we should get to know each other." Calvin leaned forward and stared at me intently with his green eyes. "Don't you?"

I smiled. That was precisely what I wanted. I grabbed the edge of our table and glanced around at our surroundings. The serving staff looked remarkably crisp. I couldn't find *one* food stain on their white aprons as they carried silver trays piled with half a dozen plates at once. And the men with their straight, confident backs and the regal-looking women with their bedazzled feather headbands decorated the restaurant.

I felt out of place.

Sure, my family was wealthy and my name renowned, but that didn't change the fact that I was probably the only one here without a Gift.

But as I shyly looked into Calvin's glowing, warm gaze, I felt my shoulders relax.

"I think getting to know each other is a *great* idea," I purred, doing my best to flutter my eyelashes. It felt awkward, and I chastised myself for trying to flirt—knowing perfectly well I was horrendous at it.

A snort and chuckle at the table directly beside us drained the color from my face. I'd almost forgotten the police officer Chief Marsh had sent along. He turned red as I shot an annoyed look in his direction, then he buried his nose into the steaming coffee mug in his hand. Strange to have coffee in the evening. At least, *I* thought so.

I took a sip of my wine, then turned my attention back to Calvin. "What should we talk about first? About our childhoods, I mean?"

He tapped his strong chin. "Hmm... What is your first memory?"

I pursed my lips. That was an interesting question. I furrowed my brow as I racked my brain for what might be my first memory. Images of rolling about in the grass as a toddler, kisses on my forehead from my parents, and tasting my first cold, delicious lick of ice cream flashed through my mind. I grinned all of a sudden as my true first memory presented itself.

"When I was two or three, I remember seeing my mother stack a pile of new books onto a bookshelf. She waved me over and placed one of the book's pages under my nose.

'Smell the paper,' she said to me."

My heart warmed as I thought back to her hushed, excited whispers.

"I remember feeling confused, but I took a huge, exaggerated whiff. The aroma of new pages and freshly pressed ink was intoxicating, and I found myself wanting more."

I squeezed my eyes shut and was almost able to attain the scent of Mother's new books even then, two decades later, and even while surrounded by the aromas of food in the restaurant.

"And did you?"

My eyes flew open, and I saw Calvin leaning forward, entranced by my tale.

"Did I what?"

"Get more?"

I chuckled. "Yes. That's when Mother decided to start teaching me how to read."

Calvin landed on the back of his chair with a thud and threw a hand to his forehead. "I refused to start reading until I was at *least* seven, much less a toddler!"

I threw my head back and laughed. I'd always had an affinity for books—ever since that moment. I claimed the experience with Mother's books to be my first memory, but more likely Mother had told me the story so often that I glorified the details and created the memory through Mother's own love for the story.

"What about you?" I said. "What's your first memory?"

Shadows fell on Calvin's face. "Ah, I shouldn't have asked you that question in the first place. I should have known you would turn it back on me." He chuckled as if he joked, but his slack expression told me otherwise.

I hesitantly reached a hand over the blue tablecloth and brushed the tips of my fingers across his hands. I just as quickly retracted the touch, still feeling awkward and shy in the relationship.

"You don't have to answer the question."

Calvin shook his head quickly and emphatically. "Of course, I should answer the question." A bit of his earlier playfulness returned in his green eyes. "We're to be married soon—I think we should know as much about one another as possible."

I smiled again. The grin was much too big, however, as I felt my eyes squint up as I did so.

Calvin cleared his throat. "I remember—well... My father was not a great person."

I drew my lips to a thin line, determined not to interrupt him. Memories of my father cleaning my scraped knees and offering money to the poor flashed through my mind. I'd never imagined someone having a father who wasn't an amazing man.

"I can remember like it was yesterday when he first hit my mother."

I gasped. "I—that's horrible."

He merely nodded before continuing, "He hated that I inherited a Mage Gift more similar to Mother's than his own. He could send his thoughts out to others and read minds, like his grandfather—"

"Yes! Your family helped my grandmother invent the gem-comm!" I slapped a hand over my mouth and winced. "Sorry, I didn't mean to interrupt."

Calvin laughed and winked at me, which sent shivers down my spine. "That's alright, Julie. My father wanted his only heir to lead the Sexton Estate with a 'powerful Gift' instead of a pathetic one like Mother's. His words, not mine."

Calvin wiped a bead of sweat from his brow and gulped his red wine.

"I was also bullied in school for my Gift. I tried to use it to hide all the scrapes and bruises I got from other children, but every once in a while, I'd miss one. Father would take sight of the stray injuries, see the tears running down my face, and would always say this: 'You deserve it.'"

"Oh, Calvin." I clutched my heart as it ached for him. "When did he die?" That was all I previously had known of the former Lord Sexton—he was no longer with us.

Calvin shifted his eyes to his lap and twiddled his thumbs in jerky movements. Something about that question made him nervous.

"Julie, is it alright if we change the subject?"

My shoulders slumped forward, and my face grew warm from embarrassment for having pushed him too far. "Yes, whatever you'd like."

"Sir, I cannot let you through! You don't have a reservation!"

Calvin, the other dinner guests, the serving staff, and I perked up at the commotion at the restaurant's front.

"What's going on?" I heard someone say.

"I'm here to see Miss Melton!" Russell cried, and then he saw me. "Julie! Julie! I have a lead!"

"Oh, no..." I groaned.

I ran my hand through my loose hair and avoided eye contact with Russell as he barreled his way past tables, nearly knocking glasses from people's hands as he ran. He waved a yellow paper in his hand above his head. Narrowing my eyes, I recognized the typeface and formatting as part of a list from one of the registries.

Shocked whispers abounded as people reacted to the words "Miss Melton" escaping Russell's loud mouth.

My heart sank, fearing the attention I would get as a Melton in public, but I was pleasantly surprised as excited cries of "Inspector Gaines!" came from about a dozen people in the crowd. It seemed a sighting of the famous inspector was better than a sighting of a Melton.

Well, he deserves the notoriety—and better him than me. I couldn't help the slightly petty thought.

Russell grimaced and tilted his hat over his golden-brown curls, muttering mild profanities. He slowly made the rest of his way to our table with elbows protruding from either side of him to protect himself from any oncoming fans.

"Let's go, Julie. I have a mage carriage waiting for us."

I opened my mouth to reply, growing angrier by the second, but was stopped as the police officer to my right stood up.

"Inspe—"

"Don't you dare say it, Patrick. Russell will do."

The officer turned beet red and shuffled his feet

on the wood floor. "Chief Marsh put her under my care, sir."

Russell rolled his eyes, and I wasn't sure if it was for the delay in him wanting to take me away and follow his lead or the officer's insistence on calling him anything but "Russell."

"I know that, Patrick. And now you are relieved." Russell gave an unenthusiastic salute, grabbed my arm, then tried to pull me from my seat.

"Wait!" I exclaimed. I shot an apologetic look to Calvin, but he seemed distracted as he stared curiously at the paper in Russell's hand.

Russell glanced in Calvin's direction, then folded his arms, which tucked the paper away within the folds of his coat.

"I'm sorry, Lord Sexton, but I require your fiancée's assistance." He directed his attention to me with a sly grin on his stubbled face. "And besides, she *is* a murder suspect. She really needs to do what I tell her to for the time being."

I rolled my eyes. "Technically, Russell, you have no jurisdiction over me. I don't have to go with you."

"Actually, miss."

All eyes turned to the gangly officer.

He cleared his throat. "Inspe—Lord—Russell is really the best. If he needs your help, I think as an officer of the law, I must ask you to go."

I clenched my fists.

"However," the man eyed Russell but seemed to quickly regret it as the former inspector shot an annoyed look right back, "I insist that I come with you. You are not a policeman anymore, sir. We need to know where she's going."

Russell frowned, but he gave a quick nod. "Fine. But there's no room for you in my carriage."

"I have one, sir."

"Stop calling me 'sir.'"

13

Russell

THE GIRL WAS INTRIGUING, AND RUSSELL OFTEN found his mind wandering to that rather than the murder case at hand. He was almost sure Miss Julie Melton hadn't killed her brother-in-law. She was too anxious—her hands constantly shaking, her eyes darting back and forth as if searching for an answer to everything. In most cases, that would suggest guilt, but Julie Melton wasn't a killer.

What's more, she couldn't make an illusion of her sister on command. Now that was a puzzle Russell was dying to solve. Julie had said she needed more time to prepare. And Russell found himself on the edge of his seat, waiting to see what would happen once he asked her to use her Gift again.

"Eugene Branch," Julie read aloud. "Former soldier from Almova. Mage Gift: inflict hallucinations."

"So?" Russell prompted. "You understand why I chose to pursue this?"

She gasped. "Wait, I met him at my engagement party. He was an acquaintance of John's during the war." She squinted her eyes shut in thought. "He had quite the scar on his face."

Her eyes flew open again, and she directed them to Russell's. "I don't remember seeing him after the few moments he and I chatted."

She tossed the registry list toward Russell's lap, but her aim was off as their mage carriage hit a hole in the road.

"And it says he's from Almova," Julie continued as Russell begrudgingly picked the list up off the carriage floor. "That's far west of here. What if he left?"

Russell shrugged, then shoved the list into one of his pockets. "The police have ways of finding people."

He glanced in Julie's direction and smirked as she tapped the top of her knee nervously.

"That's all we can do, Julie."

"I know," she whispered back.

Russell understood her anxiousness—to an extent. Her family's reputation and freedom relied upon finding the killer, but she was too on edge. It could cause some issues if Russell wanted her to stay at his side through this.

"Do you know where we're headed?" she asked.

Russell shook himself from his thoughts but continued to stare at the young woman sitting next to him. Julie Melton was a pretty thing, though her strange insistence on wearing men's clothing hid her long and elegant figure. But maybe that was her motivation. The dress and fur coat she wore at the moment for her date with Lord Sexton was much more flattering on her. The black of the material blended nicely with the dark, long locks cascading past her shoulders.

"Yes, I told my driver to take us to the Nightstar Plaza. That's where your father paid for your guests to stay, I believe."

The car lurched as they drove over another hole in the road. Julie's body flung sideways, and she landed in Russell's lap.

Julie flushed a deep red, pushed herself off Russell, and retreated to her seat.

"Sorry," she breathed.

Russell felt his heart skip a beat, but he shook his head. "Just be more careful."

The girl's face turned from red to a deep crimson as her embarrassment transformed into anger, but she didn't say anything. She merely whipped her head around, long black hair swinging precariously in front of Russell's face, and stared out of the glass window next to her.

Russell frowned. Why couldn't he find it in him to be kind to the girl? What was it about her that made him strike out?

What's wrong with me? Russell turned to stare out of his window.

It was pouring rain outside. The cold winter air was slowly freezing the precipitation and turning it into slush. Russell rested his face in his hands and pouted. He hated cold weather.

"When will we arrive?" Julie seemed to have moved past his rude comment well enough to begin speaking again.

"Do you not know where the hotel is? It's the biggest, grandest one in Pirbis North."

"I know where it is, but I can't remember how long the drive is." Julie stared at her hands resting in her lap. "I don't get out much. I spend most of my time in the manor gardens and reading books."

Strange girl, indeed, Russell thought.

"George," Russell called to the front, "you'd say about two more minutes until we arrive, yes?"

"Yes, sir. Coming up on it now."

The hotel stood on Julie's side of the carriage, and she excitedly pressed her nose up against the cold glass. Russell knew the girl was not many years his junior, but there were times she reminded him of a child. But it was endearing somehow.

"Wow!" she exclaimed, flashing a look in Russell's direction. Her brilliant, blue eyes were lit with a girlish fervor and admiration. "Look at the lights! Last time I was here, the sun was out and I couldn't see how spectacular the light gems looked from here!"

Russell gave a short nod and pulled out his flask from his coat. Even his hands displayed eagerness as his fingers danced excitedly over the cap before twisting it off. He quickly swallowed the last of his whiskey. It burned his throat as it went down, a feeling he had not only gotten used to but also craved.

Russell shook the silver flask in an attempt to release any final drops, then frowned as he found it was empty.

"So, are we just going to walk in and ask to speak with Eugene Branch?" Julie spoke, but she didn't tear her eyes away from the large building.

"Of course not. We don't want to scare Mr. Branch away—especially if he's our killer. In fact..." Russell rapped his knuckles on his thigh, "it might be a good time for you to use that Gift of yours, Miss Julie."

~

Julie

I HAD GROWN accustomed to fine things and well-kept rooms and halls, but the Nightstar Plaza was something else entirely. I'd only driven past the hotel, or waited in the carriage while Father completed business within. I found myself quite taken by the entryway made of shining, light gold tile. The hallway stretched from the five glass doors at the entrance, leading to a wide staircase at the lobby's end.

I craned my neck and gasped at the golden chandelier dangling from the high ceiling. Fake diamonds attached to thick, gold chains adorned the piece and glinted brilliantly.

"By the Moon," I breathed, "it's incredible."

"I'll be waiting just outside," the officer from dinner said from behind me.

"I was about to suggest that. Having a policeman with us might bring up some unwanted questions." Russell waved the officer away.

"Why haven't you applied an illusion yet?" Russell whispered as I moved to step the rest of the way over the threshold and into the lobby. He outstretched an arm in front of me to stop my walking any further.

"Is it like before? Do you need time to prepare?

I bit my lip. "Oh, no, uh...I'm prepared."

Russell's eyes turned from hazel to a dull glow of yellow as he studied my face. I gulped. Carefully, I brushed a single finger through my hair and drew it behind my ear. I hoped the movement would distract Russell from seeing a finger from the other hand sneak into one of my dress's pockets. My necklaces worked as long as they were on my person in some way—I only had to click the activation button of one of my devices.

I searched for one of the pendants with my hand, then repressed the urge to release a relieved sigh as I felt the button compress underneath the pad of my pointer finger. And, as always, I didn't feel or see anything, but I knew it worked. It always worked.

"Ah, a beautiful, red-haired young lady. Great choice. Looks nothing like you."

I lifted my arms in front of my eyes and saw shorter arms than my own and well-manicured nails. Red hair? Was I that girl—the maid Patricia at the manor?

"I assume you want to avoid causing a stir by hiding the fact that I'm a Melton, but what about you? At the restaurant, Inspector Gaines drew much more interest than Miss Julie Melton."

"Are you offering to put an illusion on me?"

I froze.

"Didn't think so. But even a fifty percent chance of being recognized is better than one hundred percent."

"What sort of math is that?" I scoffed.

"Now, let me do all the talking," Russell whispered, ignoring me. "If Mr. Branch is here and is guilty for some reason, we don't want him to run off."

I watched Russell as he walked forward, but his feet stumbled underneath him, and he wasn't moving in a straight line. I thought of how he had imbibed from his flask. Was he drunk?

I followed behind, forgetting about Russell as the brilliance of the lobby mesmerized me. Upon closer observation, I could see the intricacies of golden inlays on the floor, and the smooth carving of the wood along the staircase banister. The large windows on either side of us added to the picture by creating a beautiful view of the rain pattering away on the glass.

"Ah!" Russell stepped away from me and approached the counter at the side of the lobby.

I tore my eyes away from the scenery and followed Russell to the desk. It stretched the length of the lobby and was made of a fine wood stained a deep burgundy. Behind the counter stood a smiling clerk. Atop his head was a little red cap and upon his body a matching uniform.

"And how may I help you, sir? My, what a lovely couple."

I inhaled a sharp breath, ready to protest the remark, but Russell gave a slight pinch to my arm before I could say anything. I yelped at the pinch, and the clerk raised a single, thin eyebrow in my direction.

"Yes, the missus and I are quite fond of each other." Russell slid a long arm around my shoulders. He stiffened, as if nervous to touch me, but his smile remained large and bright.

I grimaced but attempted to give the clerk an enthusiastic nod.

"We would like to book a room."

Russell squeezed me a little tighter. But just that motion seemed to knock him off balance. He swayed back and forth, taking me along with him. It took a good deal of my strength to bring us both upright. And then I noticed the stench of whiskey on his breath.

This can't be good.

The clerk's smile stretched across his face as he

looked through the books and files set in front of him.

"Yes, we have one available on the third floor. That'll just be ten full pieces, sir."

The color in Russell's face drained in a second, and I stifled a laugh.

"Uh—uh, yes, of course." Russell fumbled through his pockets and pulled out a New Age Slip.

Russell's hands trembled slightly as he begrudgingly signed the white piece of rectangular paper with a fountain pen resting on the counter, then handed them to the clerk.

"Ten full pieces," Russell croaked.

With a smile still plastered on his pale face, the worker took it with a nod. "That'll do, sir. Thank you."

The short man turned to find our room's corresponding key underneath the desk. Russell peeked over the counter and cleared his throat.

"You know, we heard that a friend of ours is staying here. We'd like to give him a visit. Do you have a Eugene Branch on the books?"

The clerk rose from the floor and handed Russell the brass key to our room. "Let me check that for you, sir."

The man's nimble fingers sifted through the papers quickly. "Ah, yes. He checked out just two hours ago."

My heart sank. The one suspect that *hadn't* been a member of my family had run off, and now we had to wait for the police to find him. The hope I'd allowed myself to feel when learning of Russell's new suspect dissipated.

And it was all his fault.

Suddenly, all of the pent-up tension from the recent events came up to the surface. I ground my teeth and dug my fingernails into my palms. Who knew how much quicker Russell would have been in solving this wretched murder if he wasn't getting drunker with every passing second?

"Uh," Russell chuckled a bit, resting an elbow on the desk and leaning toward the clerk, "the wife and I only wanted to stay here to see our friend. Do you think I could get the money back? We won't be using the room after all."

The worker's smile never faltered. "No refunds, sir. It says so on the sign." The man leaned over the counter and pointed to the plaque nailed to the desk. Russell and I stepped back to read it:

"No money back on bookings of rooms at Nightstar Plaza. Gratuities appreciated."

"Do you know where Mr. Branch might have gone?" Russell said through gritted teeth.

The clerk merely shrugged. "Your room number is three zero five. Have a pleasant stay!"

Russell narrowed his eyes at the man. "Thank you."

The man nodded, then buried himself into his busy work as we retreated.

"Well, that was a waste of time. *And money*," Russell grumbled. "I am so out of practice with this type of thing."

Once we were far enough away from the clerk's earshot, I smacked his arm. Russell crossed his arms and gave me a pained expression.

"What was that for?"

"You idiot! You—you *drunk*! You are supposed to solve the murder of my brother-in-law, but instead, you are getting wasted away with your stupid alcohol!"

I moved to slap him again but instead just shook my head.

"That was incredibly stupid, by the way. You'd think someone who is supposed to be as talented as you would have thought to ask about Eugene Branch *before* renting a room he didn't want."

Russell tried to wave away what I said, but I saw the hurt in his eyes. My words seemed to affect him more than I thought they would. I felt my muscles relax slightly, but I was still too angry to apologize.

He pushed past me and marched out of the glass doors, shoulders hunched against the cold rain. I opened the door for myself and scrambled to catch up. I shivered against the chill air, pulling my thin fur coat about my shoulders and wishing I had more than fishnet stockings over my bare legs. It was hard not to feel bitter toward Russell. He forced me away from my date for a dead end and to get drenched in the cold rain. And there *he* was, stomping away in an overcoat and hat that protected him from the elements. However, I was grateful for his distraction and distance that allowed me the opportunity to deactivate my illusion of Patricia.

Careful not to slip, I chased after Russell. He stormed past the police carriage without so much as a nod and flung the front door open to his own vehicle. I waved at the police carriage, but, of course, I couldn't see through the rain if our police escort acknowledged me.

I caught up to Russell as he pulled open the driver's door and began chatting with his servant George.

Shaking my head, I pulled the frigid handle of the mage carriage's back door and slid onto the equally frigid seats. At least the hood atop the vehicle protected me from the rain.

"George, if you could just take us back to Melton Manor, that would be wonderful. And here." Russell handed the bald man the room key from the Plaza. "Once you drop us off, go ahead and spend a night in the room I reserved."

I couldn't see his face, but I imagined a smile on the man's face as he replied, "And why did you get yourself a room if the suspect wasn't there?"

Russell clenched his angular jaw. Even through my annoyance, I remembered how much my words had pained him. Russell shook some of the rain pouring from his fedora and onto his eyes, ignoring George's question, and slid into the vehicle.

"Drive," Russell snapped.

The carriage made a few worrisome noises as it started, then jerked just enough for me to lose my balance as George turned the steering wheel a few times and drove out of the hotel's paved driveway.

"What now?" I forced myself to say after we drove in silence for about five minutes. "I assume Eugene is still a suspect, right?"

"For now, we go back to the manor."

I studied the man. His fingers were inside his coat, fumbling mindlessly with something I couldn't see. A few more minutes passed and after some steady breaths, I grew calmer.

"Russell?" I wrung my hands together, starting to feel embarrassed by my actions earlier.

"Hmm?"

I swallowed. "I'm sorry if...if what I said back there offended you."

A shadow passed across his face, but he didn't say anything. He turned his gaze to look outside his window.

Deciding not to press him, I leaned my head back against the hard seats. It was well past midnight; of that, I was certain. I tapped my finger against my legs and finished the ride, wondering if Russell would allow me some sleep once we returned.

An Artist's Depiction of Downtown Pirbis North

14

Julie

WE DROVE UP TO MY FAMILY'S MANOR AND CAME TO A stop, the vehicle lurching and creaking as we did so.

"Did you ever think about purchasing a new carriage?" I inquired.

Russell ignored me and quickly pushed his door open, stumbling out. He then headed toward the manor, running at full speed. His long coat was flying behind him in the rain.

I gaped at his image as it shrank from view. "What on Dagirus?"

"Miss Melton," George gasped, "look!"

I peered through the darkness to see what the

driver pointed at, then gasped myself as I saw what Russell had run after. A tall, dark figure at the side of the building clutched a bundle of some sort in his arms. But upon seeing Russell, the figure bolted.

I fumbled with the knob to my door, then fell out of the vehicle. I hissed as my hands and knees scraped the pavement of the driveway, tearing a hole in my dress. I blinked past the cold rain and rose with a painful grunt, then sprinted in the direction Russell and the mysterious figure had gone.

My teeth chattered as the heavy rain stung my cheeks.

Where did they go? I thought, taking a sharp turn around a corner at the back of the manor.

The darkness of the sky and the freezing rain obscured my vision, but then I saw them. The inspector hadn't come close to the runaway, but he continued his pursuit. I sped up my pace, chest burning as I breathed in the cold air.

"Russell!" I cried, but he couldn't hear me over the patter of the rain and the howling of the wind.

I stopped—I had to. I rested my hands on my knees and tried to catch my breath. My hair and clothes were drenched, and my fingers were turning purple. Soon, I was able to see Russell coming back in my direction. The mysterious figure wasn't with him, but Russell wasn't empty-handed, either.

"Who was it?" I shouted out to him. "Do you—Do you think it was Eugene Branch?"

Russell shook his head, rain splashing off his hat. "I couldn't see, and then I lost him."

I wrapped my arms around myself against the cold. "What do you have in your hands?"

Russell held up his bounty with a gleam in his eye. Within his grip were a feather headband and a neatly folded piece of paper. Once I saw them, Russell quickly shoved the paper inside a pocket to protect its contents from the rain.

"Hopefully," he said, "I just found the objects that will aid in the killer's downfall."

~

I SLIPPED OUT of the bathroom and to my bedroom, a towel wrapped around my hair and fresh, warm clothes upon my person. Russell sat on the white carpet below my bed, drenching the floor with his wet clothes. His *own* damp apparel didn't seem to bother him—or, at least, his mind was otherwise distracted. The inspector stared curiously at the headband in his hands.

I cocked my head to the side and sat in front of him. I drew my brows together as I studied the white band embroidered with elaborate beading and a large feather at one end.

"Wait," I breathed. "I recognize that. I think that's Eliza's."

"Look here." Russell bent the headband to show a few specks of something red in between some of the beads.

"Is that...?"

"Blood? I believe so."

Russell's eyes were glowing again. I could never get used to that, the way they shined as he worked through various clues or made deductions was almost eerie and inhuman.

"I think the person I was chasing might have been our killer, Miss Melton," Russell whispered.

I nodded, my mouth growing dry just thinking about having been so close to a murderer. But something else happened at the same time: I felt energized as adrenaline rushed through my veins just by *thinking* back to the chase. And, as much as it might've frightened me, I enjoyed that feeling.

Russell set the headband at his feet and pulled the slip of paper from an inside pocket. "I'm hoping this might further enlighten us."

Russell slid a finger underneath the damp paper's fold and gingerly opened it, careful not to tear it. His eyes continued their intense glow as he read its contents. His furrowed brows soon rose as his mouth went from a straight, concentrated line to a shocked "O" shape. His hands went limp, and the paper dropped from his grip and onto his lap. Russell's eyes immediately stopped glowing as he placed his face in his palms.

"No, no, no," he groaned. "It can't be."

I tilted my head at the sudden anguish Russell displayed and reached for the letter myself. Pulling it close to my eyes, all I could see was a strange array of symbols and images.

I scanned the bottom of the letter, hoping to see something that resembled words, but found only an intricate stamp of a black, crescent moon. It was slightly smudged from the rain, but the image was clear enough.

"What does it mean?" I breathed.

I set the letter down and ran my hands over my face, exhaustion beginning to take over me.

"It's him," Russell whispered.

"Who?"

Russell raised his head and looked me directly in the eye, bottom lip trembling. The helplessness he displayed took me aback.

"The New Age God, Julie."

15

Julie

Morning came and went, and I still hadn't seen Russell since we found that incomprehensible letter. He had left me, demanding I not follow him, and I didn't.

I tried to sleep, but it was futile. Instead, I stared out my large bay window and watched as the rain slowed, and the sky turned from dark to light once dawn began its approach.

I allowed two more hours to pass as I thought of the New Age God. I knew of him. He was the famous serial killer of Pirbis who took up most of Inspector Gaines's focus during his short career.

And even after Russell retired, the killer's name still showed up in the papers occasionally. But that's all I knew. I didn't pride myself on staying informed on matters involving a supposed psychopath.

I didn't know the details—not about Russell's involvement, and not even about the serial killer's methods and victims, but I did know if Russell's nemesis were involved in John's murder, it would eat him up. I knew it would do just that to me.

I rolled out of bed and stared at my bedroom door, shuddering. This entire time, I knew John's murderer was out there, but seeing the note struck me like a slap in the face. Nearly every part of me wanted to curl away into my soft covers and hide from the evil. He could be close—in my own home, even. I squinted my eyes shut as memories of the mysterious figure from just hours before ran through my head.

But I had to do *something*.

I tugged on pants and a shirt and pulled out one of my long, black coats from inside my wardrobe. It wasn't dissimilar to Russell's, but the cut fit a feminine form better. I slid my arms through the soft sleeves and wrapped the coat's tie around my waist. The next step was to get enough illusion necklaces.

As a murder suspect, I wasn't supposed to leave the manor without Russell or a police escort. But I had to find some answers.

I shoved my hands deep into my coat's front pockets, fingering the cold chains of a few necklaces in each of them. Another short, silver chain swung back and forth around my neck as I scurried toward the west exit—the one I assumed the fewest people would be near at this time of day. Only an hour or so had passed since the sun rose, making the serving staff the only ones awake as they prepared for the day's meals and the manor's needs. And they would remain in the servant's wing on the opposite side of the building for the next hour. I could escape without arousing suspicion.

Head down and eyebrows drawn together in concentration, I sped up my pace and passed one corridor after another. Almost instinctively, I brushed my finger against the locket resting above my collar bone. I raised my head up, a little more confident than before as I knew my appearance became Patricia, the maid I had transformed into the night before at Nightstar Plaza. The illusion even included her uniform.

"Almost there," I whispered aloud. I could see the exit just ahead.

"Hey! Where are you going?"

My heartbeat quickened, but my subconscious

mind was faster than my fear. I knew *precisely* the illusion I needed to use even before I knew who spoke. I felt the correct shape of the pyramid-shaped pendant in a hidden pocket within my coat, pressed the button, then whirled around with head held high and shoulders rounded back just as she would.

"Ah, Clara. I mean, Lady Melton. What are you doing here?"

My shoulders relaxed at the sight of Uncle Morris, but I quickly caught myself and straightened my posture again.

"Morris." I deepened my voice by a register. I'd acquired a knack for impersonating certain voices while using my illusion necklaces—Mother's voice was one I had mastered.

"I have some business to attend to."

My uncle raised a gray brow and scratched the top of his bald head. "But you're leaving through the servant's entrance?" He avoided my eyes like he always did when speaking with my mother.

I shrugged and hid my trembling hands behind my back. "I like to change things up every now and then." I narrowed my eyes at him. "What are *you* doing on this side of the manor at a time like this?"

"I just needed a change of scenery. All of this murder stuff has me feeling depressed." Morris shook his head. "So, I've been taking walks wherever I can."

I nodded. It made sense. I would do the same if I didn't have Russell as a guard dog. This was my first moment away, and I *still* had to disguise myself.

An awkward silence ensued, and Morris shuffled his feet along the short carpet uncomfortably.

"Well, be safe, milady."

I bit my lip as he turned to leave. "Uh, Morris?"

He craned his head back but not quite enough to look straight at me.

"Please tell no one you saw me. I don't want anyone to worry—what with all that's happening right now."

Morris nodded. "Of course." And then he scurried away.

Such a strange relationship they have, I thought, turning away myself and barreling my way out the swinging door.

16

Julie

"You wanted to go to the library, Lady Melton?"

The family driver raised a quizzical brow as he shot a quick glance in my direction. The screeching of carriages in front of us made me wince as his look back at me distracted him from the road.

"Sorry!" he cried, yanking the steering wheel to pull the carriage back into the correct lane.

I dug my nails into the leather seat underneath me. "Yes, Miles. I need to go to the library. I'll only be there for an hour or two. If you could wait to take me back home, that would be wonderful," I said in my best imitation of Mother's voice.

Miles lifted a finger to scratch his hairy earlobe, but he didn't say anything more.

I sat back and shivered as the cold seat brushed against my bare neck underneath the tail I had tied in my hair. Even though my illusion of Mother portrayed a look of her hair loose and falling past her shoulders, my body still felt as if it were me.

"We're here, milady."

I dared to peek my head through the window. Wincing against the cold air, I squinted my eyes toward the tall building with its dozens of windows.

"Thank you, Miles."

I pulled the handle open and slid out of the mage carriage before he could say anything else.

As I climbed the few steps leading to the entrance, I made sure no one was looking my way to see my next transformation. Satisfied, I placed a hand inside an inner pant-leg pocket and pressed the button on the side of another necklace. I donned an image of one of Father's friends from across the country. He was no one close to Father in particular. Still, I could easily imagine Ronald's dark hair and big, gray spectacles magnifying his beady eyes, even without seeing the illusion myself. And since he lived far away, I did not have to fear someone recognizing me.

I pushed the brass door a little *too* excitedly. The metal clanged against the inside wall, and all eyes landed on my face. The receptionist at the front— bright pink glasses perched at the tip of her nose— slammed a long finger on her wrinkled lips.

"Sorry," I mouthed to her and the other dozen or so people studying at various tables with books and papers in hand.

I slunk my way to the back corner, heart pounding as I still felt eyes searing into me. It was not the time to draw unwanted attention to myself.

I sighed in relief as I found refuge behind a tall bookcase. Craning my head back, I whistled, quietly. At *least* two hundred books rested on a single bookcase, and another twenty cases just like it scattered the library.

I'd never been to the Pirbis North library— Mother had nearly everything I'd ever want to read, but she didn't have what I *needed* at that moment. The library was a maze. I didn't have any clue how the library organized their books. Was it by genre? Author? Mother liked to do it by size. And I wasn't even searching for books! I needed the archives section.

I sped up my pace, boots scraping across the tiled floor as my head darted back and forth in search of anything that looked like files or old news-papers. I walked so fast that I didn't see the edge of a long table as I turned a corner through two tightly knit bookcases.

"Ugh!" I muttered under my breath, grabbing the hip I'd slammed into the wood.

"Hush!" someone hissed from a dark corner.

Shaking my head, I looked around and sighed in relief. I'd found it—the archives. Enormous stacks of new and old Pirbis North newspapers surrounded me, gathering bits of dust from neglect, and piles of photographs dotted the stacks like snow on a mountain.

I moved over to the closest stack. "Are they organized by year?" I muttered to myself.

The smaller pile of dust on the first set of papers answered my question, suggesting the top papers were more recent and the further down the stack went, the older the newspapers were. If only I could remember the year I'd first heard of Inspector Gaines's retirement. Four years ago? Five?

My hands slid along the rough edges of the newspapers, and I pulled a few from the top of one of the stacks. I smiled at the sight of the first headline: "A New Killer Terrorizes Pirbis North." It only could have meant the New Age God. As far as I knew, serial killers weren't an everyday item.

I piled more papers onto the stack in my arms and heaved them on top of the closest table. The pile landed with a thud, releasing a large plume of dust directly into my face. I waved the cloud away, trying not to cough too loudly as the dust tickled the inside of my nose and throat.

I plopped down on the hard wooden seat and began working through the articles. I had to squint my eyes and press my nose against many of them to read the faded ink. "Killer Calls Himself 'New Age God,'" one headline read. My eyes grew wider and wider as I continued through. "New Age God Kills Third Lord This Month," "New Age God Kills Maid in an Alley," "New Age God Kills Children."

I dropped the paper I was reading before me and rubbed my eyes. This man was terrible—more so than I ever realized. I felt ignorant; I felt disgusted. Taking a deep breath, I grabbed the next article and sighed in relief to read "Inspector Gaines Takes on the New Age God Case" at the top. I moved my eyes down to the column underneath the headline:

```
After his quick solve of the
murder of Lady Norris, found
stabbed to death on the Pirbis
Express, Inspector Russell
Gaines has been assigned the
long-running New Age God case.
```

```
The chief of police offered this
statement:
```

```
"I've been wanting to assign
Inspector Gaines to this one for
a while. Not only is he clever,
but his Gift has proved its
usefulness on more than one
occasion."
```

I stopped reading the story after the opening paragraphs and scanned the bottom for the print date. It seemed Russell had taken on the case six years ago. I needed something a little more recent if I were to find out why he'd dropped the New Age God case.

Did a paper have anything on his retirement? Anything that might indicate why chasing after the killer might have sent Russell away from police work?

And then I found it.

"Amelia Gaines Becomes the New Age God's Fourth Child Victim."

"Gaines?" I blurted out loud, only to bite my tongue as another "Hush!" quieted me.

```
After the brutal murder of his
sister by his nemesis, the New
```

Age God, Russell Gaines is
taking early retirement at the
age of twenty-five.

I clutched the paper so hard it tore. I winced and gingerly set it away from me, but I was too shocked by what I'd read to look around for any suspicious eyes floating in my direction.

Suddenly, it all made sense. Russell had no intention of facing a past such as his ever again—he left the police force because his sister had been *killed* by the very man he hunted. The morbidly curious part of me wanted to know exactly what had gone down, but the nurturing side of me felt a pang in my heart for the former inspector and his family. I shuddered at the mere thought of something so cruel happening to my sister. Even just the pain Eliza was going through now with her husband's murder made my heart ache.

My fingers twitched over the article as I debated whether to read *how* the New Age God murdered Amelia. And, of course, I couldn't help myself. I shoved my face in front of the article and scanned the words.

"...one among many young children killed by his hand," one line read.

"...beaten, battered, bloodied," said another.

I shoved the paper away and clutched my churning stomach. *That poor, helpless child.*

~

OUTSIDE THE MANOR, I craned my neck up to the sky to study the sun's position. It was at least mid-afternoon. The rays of the sun, peeking through the winter clouds, brought welcome warmth to my cheeks.

I then moved my gaze to the door in front of me —the servants' entrance. This provided the best opportunity to enter without alerting anyone to my absence. That is, as long as my absence hadn't yet been discovered.

I winced as the wooden door creaked open on its rusty hinges. I wore Mother's illusion, and I prayed that I wouldn't pass the real Lady Melton on my way. But such luck eluded me.

A swarm of people rushed in my direction as I passed over the threshold. Sounds of surprised cries and a demand to take the illusion off overwhelmed me. I blinked against the dim light, eyes adjusting after leaving the brightness outside.

"Did you hear me, Julie? Take that ridiculous illusion off and answer my question!" Mother's voice overpowered them all, and she sounded angry —not a regular occurrence with her.

I shoved my hands in my pockets. I shifted my eyes downward and hoped the movement would look natural as I discreetly clicked the button with the corresponding necklace to turn my illusion off.

Upon further observation, I could see a horde of serving staff, my parents, two policemen, and Chief Marsh. The chief's lips were drawn to a thin line under his silly mustache, and he tapped straight fingers against his crossed arms.

"Where's Inspector Gaines?" he grumbled.

I raised an eyebrow. "He's not here?"

17

Russell

"Not Eliza, indeed!" Russell blubbered before downing his second bottle of whiskey.

"New Age God," he cried to no one, "you've won! I give up! I should've never taken on another case!"

Russell threw the empty bottle across his kitchen and didn't even flinch as it shattered against the wall. He watched numbly as a few leftover drops of alcohol trickled to the floor.

"Ahem."

"What is it, George? Has Lady Bilfrith from Pirbis South come to hire me for a murder that happened in her *garden*?"

"Well—"

"Or has the *Supreme Minister* found his cat killed underneath his kitchen table?" Russell jumped to his feet and barked out a laugh. "Only Inspector Russell Gaines can solve the death of the cat!"

"You're not an inspector anymore, my lord."

Russell snapped his bloodshot eyes in the butler's direction and growled, "Whad'ya want, George?"

The butler clasped his long arms behind his back and narrowed his eyes at Russell. "Lord Melton has come to call on you, but you don't seem in the right state of mind for company. I'll tell him—"

"No, no!" Russell chuckled as he stumbled up into a standing position. "Send in the man! Why not allow the most powerful lord in Osera to see my failings firsthand?"

George rolled his eyes and retreated out of the kitchen. He came back quickly with Lord Herbert Melton in tow.

"Lord Gaines," Lord Melton said with a quick bow of his head.

"I'm not an inspe—oh." Russell hiccupped. "Well, don't call me 'lord' either."

George sighed loudly, purposefully so Russell could hear, and left the kitchen to allow the two lords privacy.

"So sorry," Lord Melton said with a nod. His dark hair stuck up in various places, his eyes were puffy and red—possibly from crying—and his strong hands trembled as he spoke.

Russell poked a tongue into the side of his cheek as he studied the man—a man customarily put together and confident. But then Russell felt distracted by the unopened bottle of whiskey next to the one he'd already downed, plus the one he shattered against the wall.

Perhaps I should offer him a drink. No, I need that more than he does.

"Sir," Lord Melton croaked, interrupting Russell's thoughts, "my daughter has been arrested."

The former inspector drew his brows together. "Lady Fletcher? I told Marsh she didn't do it!"

"No." Lord Melton shifted his gaze to the dusty, tile floor and hid the tears escaping his eyes. The man had been worn thin the past few days. "Julie. Julie was arrested."

Russell perked up. "What? Why?"

The lord clenched his fists so hard that it looked as if the veins would pop out of his skin.

"It's because of you, Russell Gaines!"

Lord Melton accentuated Russell's name with a spittle of fury that made the former inspector wince.

"Oh?" Russell braved a hesitant grin, trying to maintain his usual facade of sarcasm and carelessness. "And how did I do that?"

"You abandoned her, and she tried to go out—who knows why? Maybe she left on her own to help solve the case *you were hired for*!" The man sighed, exhaustion replacing his anger as he rubbed a hand over his eyes. "The police think she was trying to run. She had—she had on an illusion of her mother when we found her."

Russell shook his head and grumbled Marsh's name under his breath along with a few other crude words to describe the oaf.

"I'll fix it, Lord Melton. Don't worry."

～

Julie

RUSSELL WOULD SOLVE THE CASE. He *had* to. And maybe he already had. I didn't know what all the symbols on that note meant, but perhaps the New Age God was the culprit. And then Russell could tell everyone that it wasn't Father, Eliza, or me. And Othos knows I couldn't kill anyone.

As I curled away into the dank corner of my holding cell in the Pirbis North police station, my only hope was that Russell would prove my innocence by solving John's murder. But no one could find Russell. During my absence to find answers at the library, he must have slunk away, too. But to where, no one knew.

I *had* to hope, though, but it became increasingly difficult as the vile smells of old food and excrement from both humans and rodents burned the insides of my nose. Even after two hours holed away in this horrible place, my nose had yet to adjust.

Darkness engulfed me, and I couldn't decide if that was a good or bad thing. Terror gripped my heart as the scuffling sounds of rats surrounded me.

The horrifying sounds overwhelmed me so much, I almost didn't hear the approaching footsteps and the rattling of keys smacking against someone's leg.

I forced my aching, tired limbs across the damp —why was it damp?—stone floor and wrapped my hands around the cold bars.

"Is someone there?" I choked out. A dim light from a corridor many feet away illuminated a few inches in front of me, and soon I saw the blurry form of Chief Marsh entering.

"Chief Marsh!" I gasped. "Please, I didn't kill him. I didn't kill John!"

The ruddy man rubbed his face. "I know that."

My jaw dropped. "What? Did you know the entire time? Why am I still here?"

"Gaines?" the chief said.

I pressed my nose against the bars, ignoring the biting chill of the metal on my skin. "Wait, you found him? Is he with you?"

"Yes, I'm here, Julie."

I squeezed my face through the bars this time, but I still couldn't see him.

"Come on, Gaines. Come talk to the lady."

I heard the heavy footfalls of booted feet as Russell approached, then felt myself smile as he stumbled into the light.

"Russell! Thank goodness! You know who did it, right? Who killed the marquess?"

Russell threw his head back and laughed as if he were mocking me. I narrowed my eyes.

"What's so funny?" I snapped.

Chief Marsh ran a hand along his ring of about twenty keys, pulled it away from his belt, then brought a single brass key up to the lock on my cell door.

My knees buckled as relief washed over me. I pulled away from the bars to avoid falling as the chief swung the door open.

"You two can talk," Chief Marsh said to Russell. "Let me know if you need anything else."

"Am I free to go?" I called after the officer as he marched away, but he didn't reply.

"Well?" I inquired of Russell. "Am I?"

"You look terrible."

I clenched my teeth at his words and ran my fingers through my ratted hair. I dropped my hands to my sides as he clumsily plopped down—hard—to the floor.

"No, Russell, *you* look terrible." He hiccupped in response, and I raised an eyebrow. "Are you drunk? Again?"

He looked even worse than before. His eyes rolled back in his head, and he flung his arms back and forth as if he were about to burst into song.

Russell winked at me in mid-arm-swinging and procured a flask from inside of his coat. "Want some?"

I opened my mouth to refuse, then looked at the unopened flask with craving. Sighing, I moved closer to him and plopped down with a thud.

"Give me that." I held out my hand, and as Russell leaned my way, he nearly toppled over, trying to shove the container at me.

"Yes, drink, Julie. Drink to the pointlessness of life!"

I twisted the cap open and complied with his

demand with a large swig of my own. The liquid burned as it went down, making my eyes water, but it was oh, so good. I dared another gulp, then another, and soon I had downed a quarter of the flask's contents. Meanwhile, Russell pulled a second silver container from a separate pocket and began drinking along with me.

"Well," I ventured to break the silence, "I don't think Father, Eliza, or I could have done it."

"Of course not," Russell scoffed. "I knew that almost from the beginning. I am also positive the person I chased a few hours ago was trying to dump his disguise. And Lord Melton wouldn't have needed to steal any of your sister's clothes to disguise himself. He would also need a vendetta against your sister to disguise himself as her, and Lord Melton obviously loves both his children. And you and Eliza aren't strong enough to have accomplished the wound in her husband's chest."

I nearly choked on my next gulp of whiskey. "What do you mean by that? Not *strong* enough?"

Russell shrugged. "The stab wound was at the front of his chest, so he most likely saw the killer coming—that suggests a struggle, and I assume the marquess could have overpowered both you and your sister. Not to mention the dark brown hair found in his grip, which further indicates the marquess was fighting for his life."

He took another swig. "And the wound was deep, which proves the immense strength of the killer." Russell gave me a sidelong glance. "That was the first thing I noticed when I saw the marquess's body."

I set the flask between my knees and rubbed my eyes with my palms. "What other things have you kept from me, Russell?"

The former inspector released a crazed chuckle and swayed to and fro precariously. I took a deep breath and held it, clenching my fists atop my thighs.

"What does it matter? Your family is exonerated! Why should you care?"

I blinked rapidly. "Why should I *care?* Someone killed my *brother-in-law* in my own *home!*"

"You were there when I was chasing the killer! How could you have done it?" was his non-answer to my question, which seemed more a thought spoken aloud.

Yes, my family and I were innocent. I tried to ignore the sick feeling I'd felt ever since seeing John's body and waited for the relief to wash over me, but all I could think about was the killer running about freely. Not only that, but it seemed the New Age God might be John's murderer. I shook my head and took another drink. The burn from the alcohol was fading, and in its place, the familiar buzz made headway. I smiled slightly at the feeling.

"You know what further solidifies your innocence?" Russell said while twirling his whiskey back and forth, making a swishing sound within his flask.

I looked at him, brow raised. "What?"

"You don't have a Mage Gift."

A sudden coldness hit the core of my very being. My posture stiffened as I stared Russell down, but he didn't even look in my direction. He took one gulp after another of the remaining whiskey.

"What?" I blurted. "How did you know? Was it —" I bit my tongue as Russell let out a snort.

"Actually, I wasn't sure if you had a Mage Gift or not, but you just confirmed it."

I searched for a reply but couldn't find one. Russell drank the last drops of his whiskey, then frowned as he pounded the end of the flask as if more drink would miraculously spill out. He set it down and stumbled over me as he reached for my half-full flask.

"I figure you use a combination of both your mother's and your father's Gifts. You must keep an object on your person to achieve an illusion, but I don't think you can do more than one illusion at a time." Russell tapped his chin thoughtfully. "Am I correct?"

I gulped. "Uh..." I racked my brain, trying to think of a way I could hold onto my secret, but Russell knew too much.

"I think your necklaces are those objects." His eyes glowed at me as he wiggled his eyebrows. "Now, you could have placed an illusion of your sister on yourself with one of those necklaces, but you still wouldn't need the clothing. Your illusion would have done that for you."

I shook my head. There was a reason Russell was the best detective in Oseran history. If he hadn't displayed it to me before, he certainly did now. I thought back to him catching me in my quarters the day prior. He must have stood there in silence long enough to watch me frantically search for the necklace with my sister's image. And asking me to apply an illusion onto myself once at the crime scene and later at the hotel might have given him more clues.

"What are you going to do now?" I whimpered. "Are you going to expose me? My family? That I'm a fraud?" I bowed my head and bit back tears. All the lies I had spent years building were falling apart before my eyes.

Russell shrugged. "Nah. It's not any of my business."

My jaw dropped, and he merely stared at the darkness ahead of him while drinking the whiskey he took back from me.

"However," he continued, "unless you're adopted, or illegitimate, not having a Mage Gift is impossible." He studied me up and down curiously. "I doubt you're non-Oseran. And I doubt even more that your mother was unfaithful to your father."

I grimaced, thinking of the years I tried to find out what my ability was.

"Intriguing. Very intriguing," Russell mused.

Silence ensued for many minutes, and I tapped my fingers against the floor as the seconds ticked by.

"Well," I finally said through tight lips, "you've solved one mystery. What about the one you were hired for?"

Russell groaned and downed the rest of the whiskey. He dropped the flask at his feet. "We're out."

"*Russell*," I snapped, "we have a killer! This could be your chance to catch not only John's murderer but also the New Age God! You chased after that serial killer for *years*!"

"Don't you *dare* mention that to me!" Russell growled. I was stunned by the change in his demeanor. "You have no idea what that self-proclaimed 'God' did to my life!"

But he was wrong. Well, sort of. I couldn't possibly understand how he felt, but having taken it upon myself to learn more of his past with the New

Age God and the death of his sister aided in giving me sympathy for the man.

Russell's scowl slowly disappeared as he shifted his eyes downward. I heard soft sniffles and thought I saw a single tear trickle down his nose and onto his hands resting in his lap.

"I'm sorry," I whispered. "Your...it was your sister, right, that you lost?"

Russell barked out a bitter laugh. "Everyone knows too much about me."

I reached out a hand to place on his shoulder but hesitated.

"Please don't give me any sympathy."

I retracted my hand. "Sorry."

More silence. I looked at the holding cells next to us and grimaced.

Why haven't we left the station yet? Can't we talk about this on the ride home? My stomach rumbled, and I groaned.

"It was my fault, you know," Russell said. "He warned me. The New Age God."

I shifted my position to get closer to Russell, forgetting about my uneasiness with our surroundings. He continued:

"I received letters from him. *Many* letters. They were all coded, but I was able to crack every single one of them. And, at one point, he started kidnapping *children*, and one body was found days later with a note nailed to his collarbone."

Russell gulped and shut his eyes. I nodded to myself, remembering reading as much from the library's archives.

"He signed them all with that Ish-forsaken stamp of the moon," he said. "The madman truly thinks he is Othos reincarnated."

The killer must truly be insane, I thought. I almost said as much out loud, but I said nothing, hoping Russell would finish his story.

"His letters would always be so cryptic. The one right before Amelia wasn't in code, but it still made no sense: 'This is too easy. You need to move faster if you don't want any blood on your hands.'"

This time, I did interject: "But what was all the killing going to solve? Did—*does* he have any plans?"

Russell clenched his jaw. "I don't know. But I didn't stop. I came *so* close to catching him, Julie. And then..." Russell choked out a soft whimper. "Then my sister—only ten years old—was his next victim."

I dropped my head. It was horrible. I felt sick just *thinking* of someone torturing a child. But I knew what I wanted to say next, just as much as I knew Russell could solve this case.

"Russell," I said, "you don't have to find the New

Age God if you don't want to, but just think: you could be closer to catching him than ever before if you just solve John's murder."

Russell continued to stare at his hands, refusing to look in my direction. I sighed, deciding to give up on encouraging the inspector, and moved to stand up. Then, I suddenly felt a sharp stabbing feeling in my right arm. I yelped, leaping up from my position and rubbing the point of pain. It felt slightly warm as a trickle of blood ran through my fingers.

I glared at Russell, who held a fountain pen he had retrieved from one of his many coat pockets. A dribble of my blood fell off the tip.

"What was that for?"

"Well, we know stabbing isn't your condition."

"You're drunk!" I growled. Then I stumbled as I had risen too fast from my sitting position.

"So are you," he chuckled, hiccupping once again.

I continued to rub the small wound he'd created in my arm. "Stabbing isn't the condition for what?"

"Your Mage Gift."

Russell rose and circled around me. His drunken self nearly bowled me over as he inspected me.

"Alcohol obviously isn't the condition, either."

I craned my head back and stared at the ceiling. "Don't you think I've thought of searching for possible conditions to activate my Mage Gift? I don't have one!"

My sympathy for the man began to dissipate as my usual annoyance for his personality returned.

"We'll see," he said. "I'm going to make a list."

I pursed my lips. "List of what?"

He pulled a notebook from yet another pocket. "Things you've never done that might awaken your Gift."

"Seriously?"

Russell scribbled something down with the pen he'd used to stab me. "Have you ever tried ingesting metal?"

"What?" I exclaimed, throwing my hands up in the air.

"I'll take that as a no." He finished his writing with a dramatic flourish.

A smile crept onto my lips. "Wait, if you're going to try and solve *my* mystery, does that mean you will continue in solving the marquess's murder?"

Russell tucked the notebook away, then clasped his hands behind his back. "Possibly. I do need the money."

I tapped my fingers against my leg. "Well, what next?"

Russell pressed his fingers against his temples and groaned. "Can it wait for just a few minutes? I have a terrible headache."

I was feeling one coming on, as well. But it was too quick for my pleasant effects from the alcohol to have faded. Mine more likely stemmed from my time spent in a disgusting holding cell. I ignored my pain and folded my arms.

"That's your own fault," I reprimanded him.

Russell rubbed the stubble on his face and narrowed his eyes at me. "Fine. I guess our next step is heading back to Melton Manor."

18

Russell

RUSSELL KNEW HE NEEDED THE MONEY THAT WOULD come from solving John Fletcher's murder. Oh boy, did he know it. But once he saw the all-too-familiar signature on that letter, it felt like his insides had been crushed in a vice-like grip. And he relived it all:

Finding his sister Amelia missing that night. His parents' wails that lasted well into the dawn. Russell searching every nook, cranny, and alleyway for the evil man who had taken his sister. And then finding her body. Her poor, little mangled body.

Russell squinted his eyes shut and pounded his

aching head with his fists. Alcohol wasn't having its usual effect on his forgetfulness.

Julie sat beside him on the floor of her bedroom, running her hands along the carpet in search of the New Age God note Russell had found after chasing the mysterious figure the night before. He looked at the young woman, tilting his head as he studied her. He barely paid attention to the task at hand as he stared.

Julie had bathed once the two of them returned from the police station. She looked much better clean—pretty even. *Of course*, she was pretty—no doubt about that.

Russell shook his head. He pushed Julie's attractiveness out of his mind. He'd been known to charm women and think about them often, but he had more pressing issues at hand.

She has *to have a Mage Gift. It's quite the anomaly*, he thought.

He racked his brain for any memories of history books relaying such cases, but all he could recall was reading of "late-bloomers" who had conditions attached to their Mage Gifts. They had to be placed in a certain situation before they could use their abilities. The situation usually only had to happen one time. And in all the records of such things, late-bloomers found their condition well before they were Julie's age.

How old is Julie? Twenty-four? That's a long time not to find her condition.

He pulled out his black notebook and studied the list of eight possible conditions, some he'd come up with himself, and others he had learned from others trying to discover their Gift:

1. Ingesting metal
2. Breathing water
3. Getting stung by a bee
4. Eating a worm
5. Jumping out of a moving mage carriage, or off a horse, out of a train. Really, jumping out of any moving object.
6. Performing on stage
7. Singing to animals
8. Long-term fasting

Russell felt he could easily test most, if not all, of those ideas.

"Russell? *Russell!*"

"What?" he snapped at Julie.

"I found the letter." She lifted the cursed piece of paper from underneath her bed and held it up to the light. "You say you can decipher the strange symbols?"

"I am particularly good at decoding the New

Age God's cryptic memos," Russell muttered, reluctantly taking the letter from Julie.

He straightened the creases on the page and stared at the symbols. He almost forgot Julie was in the room as he studied it. Russell quickly made his eyes glow as Julie inched over to look where he did. It was almost hard to remember that he, himself, was a fraud when his thoughts were occupied with thinking of Julie's secrets and lack of Gift.

"A lot of these symbols are familiar, but the New Age God created about a dozen different codes for me to solve in the past."

Russell ran a finger over the ink on the page, searching his mind for the different ciphers he had created in the past to decode the killer's letters.

"I need room."

Julie backed away as Russell spread himself on the floor. He set the letter down on the rug and pulled out his notebook from his coat.

"Do you have any alcohol in here? It'll help me think."

Julie crossed her arms tightly over her chest. "Don't you dare. You and I both know drinking does *not* help you solve cases."

"Can't blame me for trying," Russell muttered.

The images on the page had a triangular theme —almost like a pattern. Each symbol, at first glance, seemed random, but Russell noticed they all had a triangle drawn at its top, at a side, or on the bottom.

Each triangle's placement must indicate different letters or sounds, Russell mused, tapping his chin with his pencil.

The New Age God had done something similar in the past, and if Russell could just remember the cipher he'd made for it, solving this code would be easy.

The former inspector flipped past the pages with his scribbles on ideas to bring out Julie's Gift and stopped at a clean page.

It came to him quickly as he wrote out the letters of the Oseran alphabet. His memory was impeccable as he placed the corresponding symbols next to each letter. And after a few adjustments, his newly made cipher started to work for the note in front of him. He wrote the sentences in his notebook.

"This is it!" Russell cried triumphantly.

Julie peeked her head over his shoulder. Her long hair brushed his cheek. She smelled of honey. Julie read the words aloud:

THE GIFT I HAVE LOANED TO YOU WILL PROVIDE YOU WITH THE MEANS TO BOOST YOUR OWN GIFT SO THAT YOU CAN EASILY LOOK LIKE LADY ELIZABETH FLETCHER. COMPLETE THE KILL AND MAKE

CERTAIN SOMEONE SEES YOU AS ELIZABETH BEFORE YOU BECOME YOUR USUAL SELF AND RETURN TO THE PARTY. AND OF COURSE, THESE ACTIONS WILL ENSURE WHAT WE HAVE PLANNED FOR YOU ALL ALONG.

-YOUR GOD

"What on Dagirus does any of that mean?" Julie whispered.

Russell still could not bring himself to think through the newly deciphered words. All he could concentrate on was his fear that the New Age God wrote this letter knowing Russell would find it. Why else would the killer write in a code familiar to Russell?

"Inspector Gaines? You sent for me?"

Russell and Julie whirled around to the new voice. Russell hurriedly tucked away the letter and his notebook.

"Ah, Lacy. Thank you for coming."

"Laura, sir."

"Yes, sorry." He shot her a brilliant smile as he stood.

"Honestly, why does she get to call you 'inspector?'" Julie whispered through pinched lips.

Russell ignored her and approached the maid

with outstretched hands. He took Laura's arm and urged her to take a seat on the edge of Julie's bed.

"I came as quickly as I could," Laura said.

"Well, I just need you to identify something for me."

He brought a dim glow to his eyes and winked at the maid. She giggled and clapped her hands together like a child. Russell slid a hand into one of his coat's front pockets and felt for the headband. His finger brushed the feather first. It tickled his skin as he reached his grip around the rest of the band.

"Did the Eliza you saw have this on?"

Russell held the accessory up to the light shining from the dangling gem in the room. The maid squinted at it, and after a few seconds, her eyes widened as she nodded.

"Yes, yes! She was wearing that! And she had a pink dress on, too!"

Julie barked out a laugh. "Eliza would *never* wear a non-coordinating outfit. She's too much like Mother to do something like that. And that was definitely not what she wore for the party."

Russell replaced the headband in his pocket. "Well, that further proves your sister's innocence."

The maid gripped the seat of her chair and moved her head back and forth between Russell and Miss Melton.

"Really?" she said. "You don't think it was Lady Fletcher? But I saw her—"

"You *think* you saw her." Russell yawned. "Alright, thanks for your time, Lilly."

"Laura."

"Right, Laura." He winked again, and the woman bit her lip as she shifted her gaze to her hands. "Thank you," Russell said to her.

The maid continued to blush and nodded as she retreated from the room. Russell and Julie followed slowly behind.

"Where are we headed?"

Russell could barely hear Julie's question over his thoughts. "I guess going back to the crime scene is as good a place as any."

They walked together in silence. Russell knew what Julie was going to ask him next. She wanted to know every single step along the way. But no matter how hard he tried, Russell's thoughts couldn't remain on the case at hand. They switched back and forth from thoughts of his sister and the New Age God, then to Julie's curious situation.

He tried to keep his mind focused on the latter. *What situations can I create that Julie hasn't experienced before?*

Russell stopped walking and grabbed Julie's arm. "Have you ever been with a man, Miss Melton?"

Julie tore her arm away from his grip. "Excuse me?" she huffed.

Russell stepped back and tapped his chin. "I assume Calvin is the first man you've ever really had feelings for, considering the interaction I saw between the two of you yesterday."

Julie crossed her arms around herself. "So?"

"I doubt you've ever kissed anyone."

Her jaw went slack, and her bright eyes widened. "I—I—what? How dare—"

She stopped speaking as Russell moved close to her. He stared into her soft blue eyes that had a bit of a twinkle in them. His hands twitched forward as he tried to muster his courage. He felt Julie's body tremble as he ran a finger through her dark hair and tucked it behind her ear.

"Russell, what are you—"

Before she could finish speaking, Russell moved in with a speed she couldn't catch up with and pulled her into his chest. He grabbed her face and pressed his lips against hers.

~

Julie

I COULDN'T BREATHE. Russell's warm lips pushed hard against mine, and his entire body enveloped me in a tight embrace that I couldn't escape. For a split second, my eyes fluttered to a close, and my heart skipped a beat.

He continued to part my lips with his, and we stood frozen in our kiss for what seemed to be minutes. I felt myself grow lost in his touch, but then one important thing crossed my mind: Calvin.

I tried to yank my head away, pounding my fists against his broad chest. He finally pulled away, hands still on my shoulders and eyes studying my face.

"What was that for?" I cried, wiping at my mouth.

"You don't feel anything?"

"Other than your lips, n—"

All of a sudden, my vision flashed a brilliant white. I cried out and crumbled to the floor. I couldn't see anything.

"Julie?"

I could feel Russell trying to pull me up, but I couldn't move. The brilliant light overwhelmed me. And then it changed. I saw something... A child—a tall child, maybe six or seven years old. His thick, golden-brown hair blew over his forehead against an unseen wind. It was as if my mind brought me to where the boy stood. I waved my hand in front of the child's face, but he couldn't see me.

I saw nothing except the child, but he was speaking with someone.

"I figured out what my Mage Gift is, Mother." The boy bounced up and down on his toes. "Watch!" His greenish-brown eyes began to glow.

I gasped. *Is this...?*

"Is that all, Russell?" a surprisingly deep, female voice inquired. "Does the glow make you do anything? Think anything?"

I approached the child and stared into his face. He still didn't see me. His glowing eyes looked past me as if I were a ghost.

"No. They just glow. But I saw my eyes in the mirror, and I think they look incredible when I light them up!"

They just glow? I thought. *But Russell solves crimes...*

The unseen woman continued speaking:

"Russell, I love you no matter what, and I'm glad your Mage Gift has arrived, but glowing eyes isn't the Gift the son of a lord would have."

Realization dawned on me as she spoke. And just as quickly as I had been sucked into the vision, I popped back to reality. My eyes fluttered open to see Russell standing over me with a giant grin on his face.

"Do you have a Mage Gift, Miss Melton?"

I gasped for breath, unsure of my footing as I rose. "You—" I sputtered. "You are a fake!"

Russell furrowed his brows and raised his hands defensively. "Whoa, what are you talking about?" He darted his eyes about the hall to see if anyone else was around. His anxiety only furthered my suspicion. "What did you see?"

"Your Mage Gift doesn't help you solve crimes at all! Your eyes just *glow* on demand!"

Russell gritted his teeth and grimaced.

"Do you deny it?"

"No." He sighed and lifted his hat from his head to run a hand through his hair. "No, I don't deny it."

"Then why? You could be the smartest man in all of Pirbis, but you hide that fact behind a lie." My knuckles turned white from clenching my fists so hard.

"You're one to talk," Russell scoffed.

My shoulders fell. He was right. My distaste for his lies was beyond hypocritical. I had been living a farce for four years with my illusion necklaces. Sure, Russell had been pretending his Mage Gift was more potent than it was, but what really caused more harm: His lies or mine?

"But why?" I whispered. "What's the point?"

Russell's fingers twitched nervously. "We can't talk about this here."

"Why?"

He darted his eyes about and lifted a finger to his lips. "Follow me."

Russell turned quickly and rounded a corner. Taking a deep breath, I started to follow but stopped as my thoughts overwhelmed me.

"I have a Mage Gift!" I breathed, clutching my chest and feeling my lips twitch into a smile. I hadn't processed it until that moment. I didn't know how it happened, I didn't know why now, but I didn't care!

The little girl in me raised me to the tips of my toes, and I prepared to jump up and down in jubilation, but my limbs froze as I heard the heavy footfall of boots approaching. Any other day, this wouldn't have scared me, but all the talk and anxiety over murderers running about had me on edge.

Russell had vanished, so I held my breath and looked for a quick exit, but the footsteps drew near. I closed my eyes and turned to the newcomer, praying to Othos I would meet with a friendly face.

"Julie?"

I opened my eyes and sighed in relief. "Calvin!"

My fiancé beamed down at me and wrapped me up in a warm hug.

"I was getting worried," he whispered in my ear. It made my skin tingle. "You had to leave dinner so quickly last night."

"Oh," I groaned. "I'm sorry. With everything that's going on—"

"That's what I wanted to talk to you about," he interrupted. Calvin gripped my shoulders and studied my face with his light-green eyes.

I shrank underneath the intensity of his stare. "What is it?"

"What if we run away?"

"What?"

Calvin stepped back and ran a hand over his face. "We could run away and get married now! You wouldn't have to deal with the murder investigation, and you wouldn't be a suspect anymore. And face it, that inspector seems insane! His methods are ridiculous, and he's dragging you everywhere he goes!"

I slightly lost my balance, shocked by his proposal, and still recovering from alcohol consumption. "You can't be serious."

"I can't stand it here anymore, Julie. I don't like that there was a murder, and I just want to get away from it." He moved closer and grabbed my hands. "I want to get away with *you*." His eyes were unblinking and appeared haunted as he studied my lips. "And I wanted to do this a while ago."

He kissed me. My stomach did flips, and I couldn't help but smile underneath his soft lips. It all was kind of romantic. But then...there were

Russell's lips. Just thinking of them made me weak at the knees.

"I was here first," I pictured Russell saying through a toothy grin as he waved.

I had gone my entire life without having, or particularly desiring, such a physical connection with someone, but now I had kissed two men within minutes!

I pushed Russell out of my thoughts, slowly closed my eyes, then melted against Calvin's touch, shuddering as he placed a hand at the back of my neck and pulled me in closer. He smelled of tobacco, soap, and expensive scotch—quite unlike Russell, who mainly smelled of cheap whiskey. Though I was certain I probably smelled similarly.

And then everything changed around me.

A painfully bright light flashed in my vision, then darkness enveloped me. I tried to feel my way through it by blinking rapidly and outstretching my arms.

"Hello?" I called out.

What's going on? I thought.

"Ah hah!"

I whirled around to see Calvin clutching a letter. He scanned it with an eager grin plastered on his face.

"He loaned me a Gift that will boost my own?" Calvin read aloud, lowering the yellow paper and staring quizzically into the darkness. "Well, let's try it."

I tilted my head to the side, moving in closer to study Calvin's chiseled, square jaw and the line that formed between his brows as he concentrated.

Calvin squeezed his eyes shut and remained still for several seconds. I held my breath as his fists grew tighter, and his lips went into a straight, tight line.

And then his face changed. I gasped as his nose shrank and his face transformed into a delicate oval shape. His eyes turned a stormy gray with pretty hues of blue eyeshadow resting atop his lids. Even his body changed to the petite frame of a woman. He looked like... He looked...

My limbs went numb. He looked like Eliza!

19

Julie

"JULIE? JULIE! ARE YOU ALRIGHT?"

Calvin shook me. I snapped out of my vision, suddenly feeling cold. I couldn't move my mouth to reply to my fiancé. *He killed John!*

I stood frozen, not knowing what to do. Calvin stared into my eyes, worry lines drawn into his forehead.

"Should I not have kissed you?" he said, holding me up in his grip. He looked down to his feet and blushed slightly. "I'm sorry. I just—I *really* like you, Julie."

I gulped. *Should I tell him what I know? Tell the inspector first?*

"Will you meet me?" Calvin whispered, interrupting my thoughts.

I opened and closed my mouth, but words didn't even form in my mind.

Calvin clasped my hands in his, and I flinched. "I'll wait outside the manor with a carriage until midnight tonight. If you're not there, I'll take that as your answer and never bother you again."

He kissed my knuckles—an action that just an hour ago would have caused me to blush and giggle. Now, it felt like my insides were churning sickeningly. Calvin straightened and left just as quickly as he had come.

My arms splayed at my sides, and my head pounded so hard my vision began to grow blurry.

What do I do? I thought. *Chase after him? Tell the police?*

"Russell!" I whispered aloud, remembering that he had just vanished around the corner. I *had* to tell him.

I pushed through the shock coursing through my body and bolted after Russell.

∾

Russell

RUSSELL HEARD footsteps coming down the hall.

Is that Julie? He peeked his head out of the dark closet to get a good look. He had claimed the closet to explain to Julie the secret about his Mage Gift in private, but she had never shown up.

Julie ran in his direction, breath heavy and cheeks red from exertion. Russell released a relieved sigh at the sight of her.

"Where have you been?" he whispered, waving her inside.

"Sorry," she gasped. "I—I—Calvin..."

Russell pulled her into the closet and shut the door with a soft click. Reaching for a chain, he pulled it to turn on the hanging light gem and studied Julie's face. Her blue eyes had grown dark as if she saw something frightful.

"Take a breath and tell me. Slowly."

She nodded, gasping for air. It was more than the running that had her out of breath.

"Calvin. He's the killer!"

Russell's eyes grew wide, and he brought a single finger to his lips. "Shh! Someone might hear you." He placed his hands on Julie's shoulders to calm her. "How do you know this?"

"He kissed me—"

"He kissed you?" Russell couldn't help but chuckle. "You're popular today."

Julie ignored his jab, which was quite unlike her. "I saw him getting a Mage Gift. It was like I saw it with you, but this was different. It was like he was getting a second one."

Russell held up his hands. "Wait, how exactly did you see it? Your Mage Gift shows you others' Gifts?"

"Yes, but that's not important right now. I saw him read a letter about borrowing a Gift that would allow him to boost his own. Then he transformed into Eliza!"

Russell paled, realization dawning on him. He fumbled through his pockets.

"Where is it?" Russell rasped, heart pounding.

"Where is what?"

"My notebook! Where I wrote what the letter says!"

Julie's eyes grew wide. "Of course! The New Age God! The letter you found last night must have been the same one I saw in my vision!"

Russell pulled out his notebook and flipped through the pages quickly. Once he found the correct page, he brought a dim glow to his eyes.

Julie cleared her throat. "Ahem."

"Oh, right." Russell hadn't even known he was doing it. "Sorry, habit."

He stopped using his Gift, then scanned over the words he had decoded earlier:

THE GIFT I HAVE LOANED TO YOU WILL PROVIDE YOU WITH THE MEANS TO BOOST YOUR OWN GIFT SO THAT YOU CAN EASILY LOOK LIKE LADY ELIZA-BETH FLETCHER.

"This is it," Russell whispered, "it was Lord Sexton, and he obviously had help." He waved the notebook in the air, then pulled the letter out from his pocket.

"Calvin Sexton was the mysterious figure we were chasing," Russell continued. "This letter from the New Age God was for him, and he stupidly dropped it for us to find."

Julie opened her mouth to respond, but Russell continued before she could interject:

"What did Calvin see you for? Did he ask you to do anything? Say anything?"

Julie nodded, wringing her hands and flushing slightly. "He asked me to elope with him. He wants to leave tonight."

Russell raised an eyebrow. "He did, did he? Well, let's use that to our advantage." He perked up at the sound of oncoming footsteps. "Someone's coming."

He pushed the closet door open and nearly scared a young manservant out of his wits.

The servant gave Julie a curious look, then smirked at Russell before heading on his way.

Julie moaned. "Well, that'll start some rumors."

"That doesn't matter now," Russell snapped, shoving his notebook and the letter back into his coat pocket. "Come, follow me."

He had to place a firm hand on his hat to keep it from falling as he ran. Adrenaline coursed through his veins as he went faster and faster, assuming Julie wasn't far behind. Russell had an immaculate memory. He traversed his way through the halls, up the staircase, and back to Julie's bedroom as she followed.

Russell turned the knob and swiftly marched in. Julie followed as he slammed the door and locked it.

"This is more private."

"More private for what?"

Russell grinned. "I have an idea."

20

Russell

"I can't do that!"

Julie threw her arms up in the air. Her face was ashen, and she stared at Russell with eyes bulging.

"Of course you can. You are a woman. I'm sure you have womanly wiles that will appeal to your fiancé." Russell tried not to laugh as Julie scoffed at his use of the word "wiles."

"He'll see right through me!" she exclaimed. "And what if—"

Russell held a finger to his lips, but he was almost unable to restrain a boisterous laugh.

Julie narrowed her eyes and lowered her voice, "What if he *kills* me? He is a murderer, after all!"

"Flirting with him will work," Russell said. "It will distract him long enough for me to search his room." He pulled out the yellow paper once again, the letter containing correspondence from the New Age God to Calvin Sexton. "Even this one letter suggests they were communicating for a while. I have to see if I can find them. It could provide the evidence we need to trap not only your fiancé but the New Age God himself."

Russell paused. "But...don't flirt with your fiancé so well that he wants to take you back to his room."

"Stop calling him that."

"What?"

"My fiancé," Julie said with a glare. "And like I said, it won't work. It *can't* work."

"It will work." Russell gave Julie a slow wink and wry smile. "He's a man. It'll work. You might want to put something more...feminine on."

Julie glanced down at her baggy pants and brown shirt. "Ugh. Fine."

She stormed over to her wardrobe, waving Russell away.

"Please go while I change."

～

THE SENSE of urgency weighed heavily on Russell's chest like a pile of books. The Meltons had put Calvin in a lavish guest room, but Russell immediately saw what he was looking for. He had to remind himself to breathe as he rushed to the foot of Calvin's neatly made bed. The lord's briefcase and suitcases rested aside the bed, packed and ready for Calvin to grab quickly.

Russell let out a low whistle as he wiped his brow, then ran eager fingers over the brass clasp keeping the leather briefcase shut. If Lord Sexton kept letters from the New Age God with him, the case was as good a place as any to start searching.

"I thought I was done with this," Russell muttered under his breath as the bag clicked open.

He hadn't put himself in dangerous situations in *years*, and even then, he had professionals backing him up. At the moment, all he had was poor, awkward, anxious Julie Melton to flirt with and distract the killer. Russell squeezed his eyes shut, pushing aside imaginings of her stumbling over her toes and awkwardly twirling her hips. Taking a deep breath and convincing himself that Julie might be more capable than he gave her credit for, Russell peered into the briefcase. A mess of papers and files gave the impression of being placed there in a hurry.

The papers rustled loudly as Russell sifted

through them. His eyes darted to the tall door in fear of Lord Sexton walking in at any second.

"Oh, Othos," he prayed, a rarity for him. But if Othos *did* exist, Julie needed all the help she could get. "Please help Julie Melton distract that criminal for *at least* five minutes."

And then he found them.

Tucked away at the very bottom of a right-side pocket rested about a dozen crisply folded yellow sheets of paper. They were identical to the one he and Julie had found and the letters the New Age God wrote all those years ago.

Russell swallowed hard. As he lifted one of the papers, his suspicions were confirmed just by the feel of the rough paper on his skin. And thus, Russell felt no shock at the prominent stamp of a black moon at the end of each letter as he pulled them open one by one.

They are all in the same code as the one Julie and I found, Russell thought.

He hurriedly pulled out his notebook again and placed his crudely made cipher against the letters. Russell knew he didn't have much time, but he found the letter with the earliest date written across the top and brought the paper close to his face. It smelled of old ink, dust, and dull remnants of leather polish—most likely from having sat in Calvin's briefcase for a long time.

With a deep breath, Russell began decoding the words:

Lord Sexton,

First, if you have solved the puzzle to my code, I commend you. Second, I know what you did to your father. You killed him. Years ago. He abused your mother, and he despised you. But you and your mother are hiding those facts from the law. I respect you for how well you have done that thus far.

Russell almost felt compelled to laugh. *Once a killer, always a killer.*

Russell thought he lacked time to decode all of the first letter. Instead, he went through many of them as quickly as he could. He attained only bits and pieces, but the more letters he went through, the more he began to understand Calvin and his movements through the years—even why he'd planned an engagement with Julie.

Russell thought back to the lord lurking around everywhere Russell and Julie went. Calvin seemed uneasy at Julie hanging around a former inspector. It made Russell slightly suspicious initially, but he'd just dismissed it as Calvin being put off by his fiancée spending hours with another man. But then there was the insistence on Lord Sexton taking Julie out to dinner... He had been scared and panicked the entire time.

Ugh, if only I had seen this earlier! Russell chided himself.

But he blamed it on his fascination with Julie and her Gift—from the beginning, she had intrigued him, and Russell found himself trying to solve a mystery he wasn't hired for.

"This is a pleasant side of you, Julie."

Russell's heart jumped to his throat at the sound of Calvin's voice just outside the room.

"I just thought you should know how much I like you," Julie said with a slight lilt to her voice.

Russell was pleasantly surprised to hear Julie's convincing flirting, then quickly realized he had almost forgotten to find a hiding place. He ducked behind the window curtains at the edge of the room.

"Why don't we continue this in my bedroom?" Calvin whispered, almost too low for Russell to hear.

"Ish!" Russell hissed, freezing at the sound of the door opening.

But then Julie spoke again: "Oh, I don't think that's the best idea." She giggled. "We are not yet married, milord. Why don't you walk me back to my room? I need to start packing."

Russell held his breath, even as the door swung shut. He waited a few seconds before daring a peek into the room. Russell released a long breath of air, more grateful than he thought he would be for Julie's surprising hold on her killer fiancé.

21

Julie

I HAD NEVER NOTICED THE BEAUTY OF THE CARVINGS in our massive front door. It was at least five feet wide and about two inches thick, and the top of the doorway reached the high ceiling in the entryway. Father had our family crest carved into the light wood before I could even remember. The crest had an intricate torch chiseled into its center, similar to all Oseran lording families. At its right corner rested the image of a sparrow—the symbol that represented the Melton family. The sparrow's thin wings matched the wood of the Oseran torch with its intricate inlay of vines encircling its feathers.

I pulled my white fur coat around myself and shivered—not because it was cold where I stood, but because I felt both horrified and eager for what was about to occur. Adrenaline coursed through my veins, providing a welcome warmth as I braced myself to step outside.

An hour had passed since Calvin asked me to elope; another went by while I flirted with and distracted him while Russell sneaked into his room. Oh, what a mess that had been.

I shifted the red bag in my grip. It was empty, of course, but we didn't want to alert Calvin that anything was awry. I took a deep breath and stepped forward, pushing the heavy door open and meeting the chill winter outside. The rain from the night prior left a bitter air that stung my nose and cheeks; looming clouds darkened the sky, threatening rain again at any moment. My breath made clouds in front of me as I strode past the manor's entrance and searched the darkness for Calvin.

I still was shocked by what my fiancé had done. How could someone so charming, handsome, and so kind *kill* someone? And I had liked him—I really did! I shuddered at the thought of almost marrying such a criminal...meeting an evil man at the wedding bed, dining with him every day, or even having *children* with him! I clenched my fists as my teeth chattered against the cold. I didn't know how I could face him.

But I *had* to face him. It was all part of Russell's plan.

And then I saw him.

Calvin anxiously tapped his fingers against his long, dark blue coat. He paced back and forth in front of his running black mage carriage, which hummed softly as its force gems warmed underneath the hood. I halted in the middle of the driveway, mouth going dry and fingers growing numb.

It felt as though a fist had clenched the insides of my stomach as Calvin caught sight of me. A soft smile grew on his lips—the lips that had kissed me. The lips that had betrayed him and allowed me to see through his facade. I hadn't even had a moment to think about my newfound Mage Gift, and I didn't care. For now, we needed to apprehend Calvin for killing my brother-in-law and framing dear Eliza for it.

I forced a smile of my own and stepped closer, urging my body to cease shaking from both fear and excitement. I knew Russell was nearby. And not just him, but Chief Marsh and a few of his policemen were also hiding outside.

"It was getting so late that I almost didn't think you'd come." Calvin scooped my bag from my hands with one hand. He didn't seem to notice the bag was empty as he enveloped me in an embrace with his free arm.

I shuddered at his touch and prayed to Othos that Russell would come out soon to interrupt this rendezvous. Russell had insisted he found the evidence he needed, but he didn't tell me much more than that. But all *I* said to the former inspector was that he'd *better* have proof because the few minutes of my attempts to flirt with Calvin had been the most terrifying minutes of my life. And my eyes still hurt from batting my eyelashes so much.

"Of course, I came," I choked through the wool of his coat's collar pressed against my mouth.

"Well, it's daring to elope with someone, to say the least."

He shuffled over to the back of the vehicle and pulled open the small door to its compartment. He placed my bag gingerly atop his suitcase then shut the door.

"All set," Calvin said with a firm planting of hands on hips. "Are you sure you want to do this?"

I gulped but nodded all the same. Grinning, Calvin extended a hand for me to take. I hesitated. Russell and the police should have made an appearance by now.

Calvin swept me close to his chest and brushed a hand against my cold cheek. I bit my lip to keep it from trembling, but then he kissed me again. I froze, waiting for another vision to make an appearance, but it didn't happen. In fact, none of the previous feelings from Calvin's and my first kiss were present. Instead of the nervous yet pleasant butterflies, I felt nauseous. I squeezed my eyes shut as his wet mouth continued to press against mine.

Many seconds passed before he pulled away. He grabbed my hand and squeezed it in his gloved ones.

"Let us go then, my love."

My love. I grimaced at the words, then quickly glanced away. *Where are they?*

Calvin opened the passenger door at the front of the vehicle and helped me inside, but I stepped back. He raised an eyebrow and approached me, fingers and mouth twitching. His eyes darted back and forth, and he tried a forced laugh.

"What is the matter, Julie?"

I wrung my hands together, then forced myself to stop. I proffered another smile and shook my head.

"Sorry," I breathed, trying to stall, "I'm just nervous. I didn't get to say goodbye to anyone."

"We'll write to our families when we get to where we're going." He waved his hand at me but seemed equally nervous himself.

I stepped back again, searching my mind for

more ways I could stall. My boots nearly slid on the slick cobblestones beneath my feet. Just as the sky had promised earlier, it was beginning to rain again. I blinked the water off my lashes as a loud crack of thunder sounded ahead.

"And where's your mother?" I shouted over the increasing flow of rain.

Calvin's thick brows drew into a line as he shoved a finger to his lips and hushed me. "She left yesterday in one of our vehicles. We brought two here. Our driver drove one, and I drove the other. As I said, we can write our families when we arrive. You can even *call* yours if you want."

"Where *are* we going?"

Calvin set his jaw and flexed his fingers as if my questions frustrated him—no, *angered* him. I continued to retreat backward, looking for pathways around the carriage to make a run for the manor if necessary.

Seriously, where are *they?*

"We're heading west for now. But first, we have to make a few stops. And we need to get married, of course."

I pursed my lips. "A *few* stops? What type of errands do you need to run?"

"We need to go, Julie!" he snapped, rushing quickly toward me.

He grabbed my arm, and I yelped as his tight grip pinched bits of my skin.

"Calvin, you're hurting me!" I cried, digging my heels into the ground and trying to pull away.

"Quiet!" he hissed. He tightened his grip and dragged me the rest of the way to the vehicle.

I began to panic, screaming for help and thrashing at him. Calvin muttered curses under his breath and put both arms around me. Just as he moved to lift me over the step to my seat, the sound of footsteps made him hesitate.

"What's going on, Lord Sexton?"

Although Calvin still clutched me in his grip, my body relaxed at the sound of Russell's voice. Calvin released me just as soon as he saw Russell approaching from the fog and chuckled. He ran a finger through his hair and smiled at Russell.

"Oh, nothing that concerns you, Inspector. Julie is my fiancée, you know. We were just talking."

"Oh?" Russell smirked and clasped his hands behind his back. "She was screaming, Lord Sexton."

I took two steps away from Calvin and moved to stand next to Russell, but the inspector gave me a quick shake of his head. I furrowed my brows.

"Where are the police?" I mouthed, but Russell shot me a look that told me to keep silent.

The plan involved all the police coming out from hiding as well. What's going on?

Russell showed no sign of recognizing my concern.

"Well, if you are to leave, I'd like to query you about something I find rather interesting." Russell procured the crumpled yellow paper from an inside pocket—the letter he and I had found from the New Age God.

Lord Sexton cocked his head to the side. "What is that?"

Russell gave an even wider smile than before, bouncing on his toes as he pulled open the paper. "Maybe if I read its contents, you'll start to remember." Clearing his throat, Russell read in a rumbling voice:

"You should kill John Fletcher before the night of the party is over. The Gift I have loaned to you will provide you with the means to boost your own Gift so that you can easily look like Lady Elizabeth Fletcher. Make certain that someone sees you as Elizabeth before you become your usual self and return to the party.

"And, of course, these actions will ensure what we have planned for you all along."

Russell folded the piece of paper in a neat line and held it out toward Calvin. "I'd like to return it to you, for it is yours, of course."

Calvin didn't move. He didn't even twitch. He merely smiled and gave a short chuckle.

"I've never seen that until now. I don't even know what any of what you read means."

I resisted the urge to groan. *Of course,* Calvin would deny it. He didn't even react to the fact that Russell read a coded letter aloud. As the recipient, Calvin would know its contents weren't actually readable. I hoped Russell hadn't been planning on Calvin revealing himself by asking the former inspector how he'd been able to find out the letter's contents.

I looked to Russell and attempted to read his cues. I knew he must have a way to prove the lord guilty, but I didn't know much more than meeting Calvin at the designated time, then waiting for Russell and the police to do the rest. I was in the dark for all that would happen in between.

"I know, Lord Sexton. I know everything."

Calvin continued to laugh. "Inspector, I don't know what you are accusing me of."

Russell took two steps closer. "Don't call me inspector."

Calvin shrugged. "If you wish, Lord Gaines. I just don't know what you are getting at."

"You were fortunate to have charmed your way into the Melton family but equally unfortunate to learn the eldest daughter had already been married. So, you settled for the younger."

"Settled?" I scoffed.

Russell ignored me. "You wanted the Melton fortune, but Marquess Fletcher *and* his wife were in the way. If you killed the marquess, Elizabeth would still inherit the money. So, you had to get rid of them both."

Calvin threw his hands in the air. "This is ridiculous! I can't believe what I'm hearing!"

"But if the marquess were dead," Russell continued with a wave of his hand, "and Elizabeth was framed for his murder, both would cease blocking your path to the fortune. *You* would marry Julie," Russell nodded in my direction, "and *you* would be Lord Melton's marquess."

My jaw dropped. "You...you just wanted our money?"

A rush of cold anger bubbled up inside of me. My hand twitched as I debated whether or not to slap the man across his face.

"You bastard!" I screamed, clenching my fists. "All the sweet talk, the flirting... You're real charming, aren't you? Thought you'd get away with it?"

Calvin held up his hands. "I swear, I know nothing about this!" He then directed his attention to Russell. "Besides, you don't have any proof."

I could see tiny beads of sweat forming at Calvin's hairline. He was nervous. It was so satisfying to see that I actually smiled, regardless of the situation.

"On the contrary," Russell said, pulling out his silver flask. He unscrewed the top and attempted to gulp some alcohol down, then frowned. He eyed the opening of the container. "Ish, I forgot this was empty."

Calvin's left eye twitched; the smug look on his handsome face was gone.

"Anyway, I have quite a bit of proof," Russell continued, replacing the flask inside his coat.

That must mean he really did find more letters in Calvin's room. My shoulders relaxed slightly.

The next events happened in a blur. I didn't even see Calvin draw the knife. A single glint of metal flashed in the corner of my eye. Before I could move, a cold blade pressed against the middle of my throat.

"Russell?" I croaked.

"Quiet!" Calvin pushed the thin blade against my neck harder. I whimpered as the knife broke through a small section of my skin. The warm trickle of a small stream of blood fell past my collarbone and onto my white coat.

Russell held up his hands. "Put the knife down, Lord Sexton. You're only going to make it worse for yourself."

"I'm already as good as dead!" Calvin barked. "You solved it! It was me! Of course it was me! Who else could pull off such a brilliant crime?"

"Actually..." Russell let out a nervous chuckle. "You couldn't have pulled it off by yourself. This piece of paper tells us you had quite a bit of help." He waved the letter in the air once again.

The hand holding the knife to my neck lowered for a split second, but as I tried to escape, Calvin stiffened his grip on me, pressing the blade in even tighter. I yelped as it slowly cut me further. Much more provoking from Russell, and Calvin would kill me for sure.

"You will never catch him," Lord Sexton growled. "He is smarter than you, Inspector. He *always* has been."

"I said, don't call me—*Ugh*." Russell palmed his forehead. "I give up."

"What's going on here?"

The muscles in my face strained as I looked toward the new voice, head pressed against Calvin and knife still at my throat.

"Don't come any closer!" Calvin cried. He took two steps backward, and I stumbled along with him.

"Julie? Is that you?"

The incoming footsteps sounded closer, and I could discern my mother's voice.

"Lord Sexton, what are you doing?" Father exclaimed, rushing to stand by Russell.

"Julie!" Eliza chimed in, standing next to Father. She hugged her robe around herself. "We heard a commotion outside, but..." She looked at Russell after seeing the knife on my throat and whispered: "What's going on?"

My lip trembled as my entire family stood before us. Even Uncle Morris ran out into the rain, cheeks red from the exertion.

"You alright, Julie?" Uncle Morris asked.

"I said, don't come closer!" Calvin snapped before I could reply to my uncle. "I *will* kill her!"

My family's faces paled, and Mother and Eliza brought hands to their mouths, simultaneously gasping.

"Did—did you kill John?" Eliza whispered. "Is that what this is about? How? Why?"

Russell held up a hand to quiet her. "This isn't the time for explanations, Lady Fletcher."

"Leave it with just one kill, son," Morris directed to Calvin. "You don't want more blood on your hands."

Calvin laughed. It wasn't his usual, charming laugh. It sounded almost maniacal.

"I've killed before the marquess!" he shouted.

The silence that ensued was stark. All that one could hear was the falling of the rain on the cobblestones. My knuckles were turning purple from the cold as Calvin continued to pin my arms to the side. I couldn't help but wonder once again what would have happened if I had married the man.

"Oh? Interesting." Russell tapped his chin. But the way the light danced in his eyes suggested this confession didn't surprise him.

"Enlighten us," Russell pressed.

Calvin gripped a handful of my loose, drenched hair and pulled my head back even further, revealing the small cut on my neck that he had already inflicted. Mother let out a short whimper, and I could see her hands twitching as she resisted the urge to reach out for me.

"Do you really want to push me, *Inspector*?" Calvin growled.

I squeezed my eyes shut, almost certain this was my end. I didn't know what Russell had planned at that point, but I knew it wasn't working.

"I'm taking her with me," Calvin said. "One step, I kill her."

My family stood, helpless and shivering in the rain, as Calvin dragged me toward the carriage and shoved me into the passenger side. He maneuvered himself over my lap. I groaned as his knee jabbed my ribcage as he positioned himself behind the steering wheel without losing a second of the knife at my throat.

The force gems roared as Calvin slammed a foot on the acceleration pedal. My lip trembled as the vehicle lurched forward. Calvin had one hand on the wheel, and the other hand still held the blade at my neck. Regardless, I attempted one look back toward Melton Manor. Why hadn't the police shown up? Why had Russell provoked Lord Sexton so?

What were you thinking, Russell?

22

Russell

"WE'RE JUST GOING TO LET HIM TAKE HER?" LORD Melton cried above the skidding sound of Calvin's vehicle sliding as it quickly turned out of the slick driveway.

Russell ignored the infuriated questions from the Melton family as Lord Sexton drove away with Julie.

"Now!" Russell cried.

Suddenly, out of the damp darkness of the rainy night, a second vehicle inexplicably appeared, parked directly behind Russell. The Melton family stumbled backward in surprise.

"What? Where did that come from?" Morris Melton shouted with a hand on his balding head.

"Really, we are *all* Oserans," Russell said. "Are you not used to the variety of Mage Gifts out there? Chief Marsh can make anything he touches and its contents invisible."

Chief Marsh waved a stubby hand through the driver's side window. "Hurry on, Lord Gaines! We'll lose 'em!"

Russell tipped his hat at the Melton family. "I will bring Miss Julie back."

Russell then promptly leaped across the cobblestones and pulled open the passenger door. He hopped into his leather seat and slammed the door shut behind himself.

"Go," he urged.

Chief Marsh flipped the brass switch to the right of the steering wheel, activating the vehicle. Then, almost like he did this every day, Marsh sped the carriage forward and started his pursuit.

The Meltons leaped out of the way, their faces scrunched up in worry as Russell, the chief, and two other policemen sitting in the back were on their way.

It took mere seconds for their vehicle to catch up with Lord Sexton's.

"Be sure to stay far enough behind where he can't see us," Russell said.

"You think I've never done this before?" Marsh snapped, slowing down just enough so the dark automobile ahead was barely more than a shadow.

Russell shot a quick look to the backseats and gave a hesitant smile at the men occupying them. They nodded in return, hands poised above the force canes at their hips.

"I said not to bring anyone else," Russell muttered through tight lips.

"We're not about to go in on a mad killer without any backup, Gaines!"

Russell slid down into his seat and groaned. The two policemen in the back snickered, and Russell rolled his eyes.

"So, why couldn't we have arrested him sooner?" Marsh said while making a sharp turn and skidding around a corner of the windy road, almost losing Lord Sexton as he turned left down a street well-lit by a dozen or so lamp poles on either side.

"Go back even further!" Russell said, snapping back upright. "We don't want him to see us!"

Marsh clenched his jaw, which made his curly mustache fall over his thin lips. "Answer my question, Gaines."

Russell hesitated. He didn't know how Marsh would react if he knew Lord Sexton was working with, more likely *for*, the most notorious serial killer in Pirbis history—perhaps even all of Oseran history.

"Gaines? You're using police time and resources to go off on your own little adventure. The least you can do is shed some light for me."

The two men in the back snorted in agreement.

"Well..." Russell paused and clasped another of Lord Sexton's letters in his pocket that he had stolen from Calvin's room. It summoned Calvin to meet the New Age God. After the decoding, Russell found it to say:

THE USUAL PLACE. AFTER MIDNIGHT TONIGHT.

SIGNED, YOUR GOD.

Russell took a deep breath. "I am *hoping* Lord Calvin Sexton is meeting with our dear old friend, the New Age God."

~

Julie

CALVIN HAD long since removed the knife from my throat, but to make certain I wouldn't try to fight him, he kept the gleaming blade in his grip and continued to point it in my direction. His other hand balanced the steering wheel. He clutched it so tightly, I could see the veins in his fist rising underneath his quickly paling skin. Calvin's eyes darted back and forth along the empty roads, and he licked his lips repeatedly.

I moved my eyes back to the road as well. It was lit, unlike the backroads near Melton Manor. That had to mean we were nearing the heart of the city. But why would he go there? Policemen were always flocking the area, and it made no sense for Calvin to take such chances.

"Where are we going?" I dared to ask.

"Quiet!" Calvin snapped. "None of this was supposed to happen."

The hand holding the knife began to tremble. I inched a little closer to the window on my right and gazed out as the empty roads transformed to the beginnings of the heart of Pirbis North. A multitude of towering buildings and lights shining in the hundreds of windows came into view. It was beautiful, especially with mountains towering behind it all like a mysterious shadow.

I didn't travel to the city much—I tended to avoid anything that didn't involve reading a book and enjoying solitude outdoors in the manor's gardens. But I always found myself in awe when seeing the many streets, buildings, parks, and restaurants. Just to think that thousands of individuals in one city were living lives entirely outside my own was an astounding concept.

I tried to enjoy it. I wasn't sure if these would be my final moments. My captor was growing more and more unstable and frantic as each second ticked away. I stole a look in Calvin's direction. He bit his bottom lip so hard a trickle of blood stained his white teeth and dripped down his chin.

We drove through the center of the city, still bustling about with drunk women in short dresses and chin-length hair laughing and giggling with equally drunk groups of men. We even passed a few dark mage carriages with the word "Police" painted on the sides. Each time we passed a patrol vehicle, Calvin stiffened up further.

Once we reached the outskirts of the city, Calvin drove much slower than before, his neck craned out as he concentrated on the scenery around him. The buildings and townhouses were changing to older buildings and homes.

"I think this is it," he muttered to himself, jerking the steering wheel to the right and pulling in beside a rundown storehouse.

I squinted through the rain to get a better look. The storehouse with its hatch roof and wooden walls most likely had been a building that stored foods and products meant to be shipped across the country. That is until factories increased in numbers after Grandmother invented the mage carriage.

Calvin stopped the vehicle.

"Get out. Slowly."

Calvin brought the silver blade close to my nose. I held up my hands, then pulled the door handle next to me. I stumbled out of the carriage backward as Lord Sexton followed me through the vehicle on hands and knees. He then scrambled out the passenger side, his dark boots splashing in a puddle.

"Go inside first. And don't try anything—I'm right behind you."

I nodded and headed down the overgrown path leading to the building. Calvin poked the tip of the blade into my lower back.

"Faster," he growled.

This is it. This is how I die. Alone in an abandoned storehouse by the hand of my crazed fiancé.

At the entrance, its white paint was chipping, and the door's wood was rotting away.

"Open it," Calvin said, pushing the knife a bit harder into my back.

I lurched forward as the blade poked through my clothes enough to break skin. I reached for the handle on the door, but it fell away as I touched it.

Sighing, I slammed a shoulder into the door. Calvin and I jumped back as it fell off its hinges, creating an opening to pass through.

Lord Sexton repositioned the knife at my back before I could move—not that I had much hope of running away. Calvin was well-built. I was fit, but I knew he could still overtake me.

"What are we doing here?" I whispered as we entered. I lifted my trembling chin to convince myself I could be brave in the face of my inevitable demise.

The room we entered was empty, save for a stool in its center; the only light came from the moon shining through the gaping hole we'd left in the front door.

"He's supposed to be here!" Calvin grabbed my arm and shoved me forward. "Where is he?"

"Who?" I demanded. I was fed up with all the mystery. But even as I said it, a creeping gut feeling told me I already knew who he was coming to see.

Still gripping my arm tightly, Calvin lowered the knife at my back and pulled me with him as he stumbled through the darkness. I heard the jingle of a chain hitting Lord Sexton's hand. He pulled the chain until it clicked, and then the room flooded with bright yellow light from a light gem dangling from the ceiling.

Seeing the building covered in light left no

greater impression—it was a small, dusty space with a stool at its center. But there was one difference: now I could see a neatly folded yellow piece of paper resting on the seat of the chair.

Calvin yanked me forward, placed the knife inside a jacket pocket, then scooped the paper into his hand. I winced as the fingers in his other hand tightened around my arm as he read. I could already feel the bruises forming.

Calvin howled in despair and tossed the letter aside. He released my arm and covered his face with his hands.

"I have disappointed him!" he cried. "I disappointed my God!"

He cursed himself and slammed his fists into his forehead. I took the opportunity to rush over to where he had thrown the letter. It wasn't in code like the others—it was as if the contents were meant for the entire world to see. It read:

MY SERVANT,

YOU HAVE FAILED ME. IT IS TOO DANGEROUS FOR ME TO MEET WITH YOU. YOUR IDIOCY HAS MADE IT NECESSARY FOR ME TO CEASE ALL OUR INTERACTIONS. YOU WILL BE CAUGHT.

-YOUR NEW AGE GOD

I brought a trembling hand to my mouth as I saw the signature at the note's end with the neat crescent moon stamp right beside the word "God."

"He was here," I breathed.

I clutched at my heart as it nearly pounded out of my skin. All of a sudden, I wasn't scared of Calvin anymore. I was afraid of the serial killer who likely had been lurking in the shadows.

The sudden bursting of what was left of the door made me scream. I closed my eyes shut as the door continued to crack open.

"Miss Melton, thank goodness you're alright!"

My eyes flew open, and my knees went weak once I saw who the newcomers were. Two tall policemen rushed for Calvin and restrained him. He thrashed against them and cried out for "God" to save him.

Chief Marsh sprinted to me, his midsection bouncing as he did so. He grabbed my shoulders and searched my face. I blushed at his sudden concern for me.

Slow, heavy footsteps entered the room after the police, and I knew who it was without looking.

"Where is he, Lord Sexton?" Russell bellowed.

Calvin merely glared back with a crazed look in his green eyes. His usually suave hair fell in unkempt clumps in front of his face.

Russell stalked his way over the dirty floor and

pressed his nose right into Calvin's face. "Where is your master? Where is your supposed 'God'?"

Calvin drew his face back, teeth clenched. Then he spit. The saliva went straight into Russell's eye, but he didn't even flinch. Russell grasped the collar of Calvin's shirt and pulled him in. Lord Sexton's eyes bulged as he began to choke from the hold. The two policemen shouted out in protest as they tried to pull Calvin back.

"Gaines!" Marsh snapped. "Pull yourself together! There will be plenty of time to question him!"

Russell's usual calm (sometimes drunk and a little too care-free) behavior was absent. In its place stood a new, darker Russell. I had seen a glimpse of it when we first found that letter a couple nights ago, but this was...intense. He glowered at Lord Sexton, fists clenched and face so tight the muscles in his neck pulsed.

"Gaines," Marsh said, lowering his voice, "leave it be for now."

Russell drew his head back, then released his own spray of spittle. It landed on Lord Sexton's cheek. Calvin cried out in disgust.

"People who work with that *monster* in any way can rot in the void with Ish for eternity," Russell hissed.

"Uh, Gaines? I think you'll want to see this."

I hadn't even noticed the chief pull Calvin's latest letter from the New Age God from my grip, but his eyes were not scanning the front. I gasped— I'd missed an entire paragraph written on the back!

Russell shoved Calvin aside, making the officers holding him stumble. He stormed over and ripped the yellow paper from Marsh's outstretched hand. He began to read, shadows drawing into his cheeks and eyes darkening as he did so.

"What does it say?" I whispered.

Russell then promptly turned on his heel with the letter still clutched in his hand. He stalked away from the storehouse, coat flying behind him like dark wings as he escaped into the night.

23
_____

Russell

WE'RE IN FOR SOME FUN, INSPECTOR GAINES! NOT
EVEN YOUR EYES CAN SEE WHAT I HAVE PLANNED
FOR THE TWO OF US.

RUSSELL MULLED OVER THOSE WORDS AGAIN AND
again, which just made him angrier. The New Age
God treated Russell like a puppet, and it made
Russell want to scream. And why were there only
certain letters the killer chose not to put in code? In
Russell's experience, it was as if once the New Age

God felt he'd won, he didn't feel the need to play deciphering games anymore.

But one thing brought Russell a touch of optimism: the killer didn't know the inspector's "powerful" Mage Gift was a farce. At least Russell knew, even if it was just in his own mind, that he had some advantage on the psychopath. And that the killer didn't, in fact, have some sort of omniscient knowledge.

Russell ran his eyes over the pile of papers in front of him. With Russell's direction, Chief Marsh had a few of his men search Calvin Sexton's things after he was taken to the Pirbis North Police Department. They retrieved the other letters from the New Age God where Russell had left them.

Russell thumbed through the stack of letters for the dozenth time that hour, hoping for a clue—a small clue, *any* clue—as to who the New Age God was. He had long since deciphered all the coded letters, but none of the papers before Russell revealed any hint to the clues he desired.

Sighing, Russell pulled his notebook closer and pored over the words from Calvin's first letter again —he had them memorized by now, but Russell didn't want to miss *anything*. He brought the corresponding letter next to his notes. Maybe there was a secondary code written in between the lines, an intentional smudge...something!

I KNOW WHAT YOU DID TO YOUR FATHER. YOU
KILLED HIM. YEARS AGO. HE ABUSED YOUR
MOTHER, AND HE DESPISED YOU. BUT YOU AND
YOUR MOTHER ARE HIDING THOSE FACTS FROM THE
LAW. I RESPECT YOU FOR HOW WELL YOU HAVE
DONE THAT THUS FAR.

Russell had concentrated on those words the most, as if there would be more clues in the very first letter. And if he could find those clues, maybe he could piece them together with the other letters. Russell took a quick sip of the glass of water that had long since grown warm since he entered the empty interrogation room. He continued reading the letter:

I AM NOT REACHING OUT TO BLACKMAIL YOU.
HOWEVER, IF YOU CHOOSE NOT TO WORK WITH ME,
I MIGHT TURN TO THAT. BUT I HAVE A PROPOSAL
YOU CANNOT REFUSE.

The letter was signed, "New Age God." Other letters had the signature, some did not, but all the papers had the usual crescent moon stamp. Russell's eyes tore through his notes and the symbols written on this specific letter again: He scanned what the serial killer had planned for Calvin, all the way up to Lord Sexton charming his way into the Melton family and betrothing himself to the youngest daughter. And then there was the plan to murder Marquess Fletcher.

JOHN FLETCHER'S DEATH IS A SITUATION BENEFICIAL TO BOTH YOU *AND* ME. YOU WILL BECOME HEIR TO THE MELTON FORTUNE AND ESTATE IN ADDITION TO YOUR OWN, AND MY OWN NEEDS WILL BE MET.

"What needs?" Russell muttered aloud. "Why did the New Age God need the marquess dead?"

Russell pushed the letters away and placed his face in his palms, biting back frustrated and tired tears. Russell always came close. *So* close, yet constantly failing to catch the man who had ruined his life. And he felt more confused now than ever before.

Could the New Age God *really* lend his Mage Gift? If so, how was he able to lend a Gift that strengthened Lord Sexton's own ability? But by that logic, he would have to have *two* Gifts!

Russell pounded at his forehead. "He *could* have Melton gems," he muttered to himself. "Maybe he copied a Mage Gift and loaned it to Lord Sexton."

The New Age God's crimes used to be so random—his motive and victims would always change last-minute right before Russell felt close to *something*. And now, the specificity of his targets made things even worse. Even the killer's self-proclaimed title made no sense. What was he doing that would make him the new Othos? What was his goal?

"Ugh!" Russell cried, throwing himself out of the chair and pushing the table aside.

If the New Age God was using Melton gems for his own purposes, that was terrifying. Not only could he use Melton gems made by Lady Melton, but others (possibly as evil and smart as he) could follow. That made the world not only more dangerous but a lot more complicated.

"Gaines? He's ready for you."

Chief Marsh poked his round head through the tiny crack in the open door. The little glass window at the top of the wooden door made the chief's plump torso visible as well.

Russell nodded and moved toward Marsh. "Yes, thank you."

"You know, this is actually against regulation. I know I allowed you to speak with Miss Melton while she was in here, but you're not a policeman anymore. I shouldn't allow you to speak with a convict unattended in the department building," Marsh whispered as he guided Russell down the narrow hall.

"I know," Russell said.

"But the only reason I'm letting this happen again is because..." Marsh paused and gave Russell a quick side glance. "Because the New Age God is yours to condemn. And I want to give you any chance to find the bastard."

Russell didn't reply, his eyes remaining on the path before them as they passed five or so interrogation rooms—some held suspects for questioning in various crimes. The grating shouts and cries of innocence blared uncomfortably in Russell's ears. A rush of memories flooded his mind: the smell of freshly polished police boots lingering in the hallways, and the criminals' pleas were painfully nostalgic. It made him think of what once was before his sister's death—the joy and excitement of law enforcement. Now, Russell would never feel that again. He would never catch the New Age God. He wasn't even sure he wanted to. However...

Russell recalled the adrenaline rush when chasing the marquess's killer—the chase, the clues, and Julie. She was a fascinating young woman, for sure. And the kiss had been... No, it had just been a kiss. A kiss to help solve a mystery. And her newfound Mage Gift could prove quite helpful in various situations. He was intrigued by her Gift and wondered what the limits were. Did she *have* to *kiss* someone to activate it? There was so much more to consider.

"Here we are." Marsh held up a hand to halt Russell.

They had reached a small corridor that contained a handful of holding cells used to detain suspects and criminals before they were proven guilty and taken to the Pirbis North Jail. The innocent were allowed to go home.

The cells themselves were cruel and unusual punishment. The floors were hard and damp without a single chair or mattress. Each cell had a bucket for relieving oneself, and you just had to hope no one would watch you. At least women were kept in a separate group of cells at the other end of the building. The Pirbis police weren't *that* cruel.

"Miss Melton had a rough time here," Marsh said with fists on his hips. "She was only held for a couple hours, but it's no place for a lady." The chief tapped a furry lip thoughtfully.

Russell nodded, barely hearing Marsh as he surveyed the dimly lit cells and peered through the iron bars for Calvin Sexton. His eyes passed over a few other criminals. The darkness permitted Russell to see only their angry, glaring teeth.

"He's over here." Marsh nodded his head toward the cell at the far corner.

Huddled within the shadows of the cell sat Lord Sexton. He wrapped his long arms around himself and clenched his square jaw as he locked eyes on the former Inspector Gaines. Russell looked straight back at the man, unwavering.

"Five minutes," Marsh emphasized. "That's *it*."

Russell's eyes remained on the lord as Chief Marsh's footsteps faded away. He then promptly strolled over to Lord Sexton's cell. Hands clasped behind his back, Russell clicked his tongue.

"Look at you," he chided, "all locked up and alone. Not what you thought would happen, huh?"

Lord Sexton bared his teeth at Russell. "What do you want?"

"You know what I want." Russell pressed his nose up close to the wide bars. "I want your so-called 'God.'"

"He *is* God!" Calvin stormed, leaping up onto his feet and running at the bars. His hands slammed into the metal. The clanging sound of the impact echoed around the corridor for a good few seconds.

"Agree to disagree," Russell countered with a small smile. "Who is he, Lord Sexton? Why are you protecting him? You've already been caught. Soon, they'll transfer you to the jail and have your Mage Gift stripped from you."

Russell leaned in so close that he could feel Calvin's breath on his face. "You have nothing left to lose. Might as well drag him down with you."

Calvin clutched at his cell bars, but his hands kept slipping from the sweat on his palms. "I never saw him!" he barked. "Even if I did, I would *never* tell you. He's going to change Osera for the better, and then after that, he will change all of Dagirus. You'll see."

Every muscle in Russell's body tensed as he clawed at Calvin's dirtied white shirt and pulled the lord up against the bars so hard that Calvin yelped in pain.

"I *will* catch him," Russell hissed through gritted teeth. "And I *will* send him to the void where he came from."

And Russell meant every last word. Fury roared within his gut as he clutched Calvin in his hands and stared into the pathetic man's moist eyes.

"Mark my words," Russell whispered.

He pushed Lord Sexton away and watched, satisfied, as the man stumbled, fell, and scraped his hands on the stone floor.

"Did you hear that, New Age God?" Russell muttered under his breath before turning and leaving Calvin Sexton in his dust. "You have not won yet."

24

Julie

It felt strange not to have Russell dragging me about to follow various leads and clues. His presence at the manor had only lasted for just over two days, but his absence lingered stronger than I might have thought. But I felt insane and unreasonable for thinking such things. I'd been surrounded by danger and fear for hours on end—there had been a *murder* in my own home, I had been kidnapped and nearly killed by my fiancé, but...it all had been somewhat thrilling.

I sat on the edge of my springy mattress and kicked my bare feet back and forth across the rug.

Everything seemed dull after the events of the week. Of course, things would never be the same at Melton Manor. My sister had retreated to the room given to her and John for their visit—a short stay turned indefinite for my poor sister.

I wanted to comfort Eliza. A pregnant widow accused of killing her husband must be traumatized in ways I couldn't imagine. She mourned not only the loss of her husband, regardless of the issues they were facing in their marriage, but also the loss of what her life could have been if her child still had a father.

I got up and began to roam the length of my room. It was well into the morning, and I still stood undressed with just my short robe wrapped around my underclothes. I was concerned for my sister, but I also had been taxed by the events of the past few days. Even so, my thoughts continued to return to what my Mage Gift seemed to be.

I stopped in front of my large bay window and stared at the dead grass reflecting the yellow of the sun's rays. I rubbed my aching temples and groaned.

"Should I tell my family?" I whispered to myself.

That had been the main question on my mind in the past few restless hours. The logical answer was to tell them. But so many things about my Gift remained a mystery. For instance, if I had to kiss someone every time I used my Gift, then I would just forget about it altogether. And I didn't like the idea of explaining to my family that I discovered my Mage Gift by kissing two men within a few minutes.

My heart lurched as a quick rap on my door interrupted my thoughts.

"Yes?" I called, clutching my robe and chuckling at myself. The events of the past week had me a bit jumpy.

The door creaked open an inch and revealed a thin stream of light from the hallway and into my unlit room. My mother's blond head appeared.

"Dear, Inspector Gaines is here to collect the rest of his payment. But he also said he wished to speak with you."

"It's not Inspec—" I stopped myself. "I'll be right there. I just need to get dressed."

∽

"AH, JULIE." Father beamed at me from behind his desk as he procured a stack of New Age Slips already signed. Russell sat on the other side of the desk, his eyes growing wide as he saw the money.

"I'm glad you could make it," Father said. "We are all so grateful to you, Russell." Father winked at him, proud of himself for not calling the man "Inspector" or "Lord Gaines."

Russell offered a smile of his own, and he took the stack from my father with an appreciative nod.

"I'm just glad it's over," he said.

Father bowed his head. "Yes, we all are."

A moment of silence ensued among the three of us as we all thought back to the past few days. Then Father clapped his hands, startling both Russell and me.

"I'm determined not to dwell on the past, hard though it may be. I wish we could thank you with more than just a pile of money!"

Russell looked as if he might laugh. "Oh, Lord Melton, this is thanks enough. Trust me."

Father waved his hand. "Nonsense. There must be something."

He pressed the tips of his fingers together and pursed his lips, then rested his eyes on me. A smile broke through his bearded face.

"Of course!" he cried with a slap of his palm against the desk. "Julie here is still in need of a betrothal. You know, since..." Father drifted off and winced. "Let's not talk about that. But you two would make a great match, I think!"

My arms and jaw went slack. "Father!"

"Oh, I'm sorry, Julie. Of course, only if *you* wish to marry him."

Russell threw back his head and barked out a laugh. "No, my lord, that is quite alright."

I cleared my throat. "Uh, Mother said you wished to speak with me, Russell?"

"Oh, yes!" Father bounded from his armchair and gave Russell a quick nod. "I will leave the two of you alone. Maybe both of you will change your mind about my proposal eventually."

"*Father*," I said again through gritted teeth.

He chuckled and slid out and away from his desk, then left through the door. Russell shook his head, chest shaking as he continued to laugh.

"Maybe your father has a point about what a good match you and I would make."

I rolled my eyes. "Still as infuriating as ever, I see."

Russell arched his back in his chair and yawned as he stretched. "I will never change."

I laughed a bit at that. His odd behavior was starting to become endearing to me. Strange.

"What did you need?"

"Oh, I need a lot of things." Russell rose from his chair and strolled the length of the room with hands behind his back. "Lord Melton is quite an organized person, isn't he?"

I studied my surroundings along with him, taking in the meticulously set furniture, the clean floor, and the perfect, straight lines the papers on Father's desk made.

"He's always been that way," I replied, folding my arms.

Russell remained silent, and I found myself tapping my foot quickly against the rug with both impatience and anxiety. There was a question on my mind that I'd been wanting to ask him ever since learning what his Gift truly was.

"Uh, Russell?" I squinted my eyes shut in fear of him refusing to answer the question that had been nagging at me. "Why hide your investigating skills —your intelligence—and pretend it's your Gift that helps you solve crimes? I mean, isn't being smarter than everyone else something we all wish to attain?"

"I'm half-Oseran."

He said it so nonchalantly that I almost didn't feel the shock that should come with such a revelation. "But your father...your father was Lord Gaines, and your mother, Lady Gaines?"

Russell shook his head and ran a gloved finger along the study's brown wallpaper. "As far as the world knows, yes, I am heir to the Gaines estate. But my mother had an affair with an Ufith immigrant, and I was the product."

Russell turned his face to me, and suddenly, surprisingly, I could almost see the Ufith qualities in his face—the slightly pointed ears, the angled jaw, the thick, curly hair...

"You didn't want to disgrace the family name

with a weak Gift, so you played as if it was better than it is," I whispered, realization dawning on me.

"You know, Julie, you proved yourself quite useful," he chirped, changing the subject.

I pursed my lips, not wanting to stray from the topic, but I respected the man enough to allow him to talk about his birthright when he desired to.

"Quite useful *how*?" I replied.

"I didn't solve this crime. *You* did." Russell turned his attention to me and pointed a single finger in my direction.

I laughed. "How? By kissing Lord Sexton, then promptly getting kidnapped?" I reflexively brought a finger to the fresh cut in my neck from Lord Sexton's blade.

"Exactly!" Russell clapped his hands once. "Your...vision, as you call it, was the clue I needed to capture the marquess's killer."

"That's just it!" I cried. "How did that happen? I've kissed my mother and father before, but I've never had such a vision. Does it have to be..." I paused and lightly touched my lips with a hand. "On the lips? That's a *ridiculous* condition to activate my Gift."

"Ah," Russell held up a finger, "I've thought of that."

He fumbled for a few seconds through his coat pockets. It wouldn't have surprised me at this point if he'd had a cat hiding in there. He procured something small and held it up to the light. I squinted my eyes to see it better. It was a ring—a thin, golden band that glinted prettily against the yellow light from Father's lamps.

"What's that for?"

"Kiss it."

"What?" I scoffed. "You can't be serious."

Russell stomped toward me, grabbed one of my hands, then shoved the piece of jewelry into my palm.

"Kiss it," he demanded.

Sighing, I brought my hand up to my face and looked at the ring resting in my palm.

"Here goes nothing," I muttered.

I licked my lips, then pressed them against the cold metal. I gasped as I was almost immediately swept into darkness.

It's happening again.

I searched my mind for any sign of light or image like before, and then it came: a young boy of maybe twelve perused through an enormous stack of books.

"This is amazing," he said, flipping through his third book from the stack within seconds. "I can read the entire thing in just a few blinks!"

I stared in awe as the child giggled and sped his way through the books in front of him. Then, just as quickly as I'd been enveloped in the vision, I was brought out of it. I stumbled slightly, but Russell caught me with an arm.

"Did it happen again?" Russell gripped me tightly in anticipation. His hazel eyes turned yellow as he made them glow.

"Why do you keep doing that?" I said. "I know your secret, remember?"

Russell let go of me and laughed. "It's a habit. But did it work?"

I nodded, feeling a smile of my own appear. "It's incredible! I saw a boy learning of his Mage Gift—just like when I saw you and Calvin."

I pulled the ring to my eyes. "Why this ring?"

"It belongs to my butler, George. You see, I have a theory. It's a working theory, but I think I can figure it out. Let's just hope you don't have to go around kissing things to activate your Gift. It might have something to do with saliva, or maybe the emotional feeling you got from kissing me was the condition that activated your Gift."

I blushed.

"Or something we can't even see. I'll work on it."

I cocked my head to the side. "You'll *work* on it?" I threw my hands up in the air. "I've been waiting my entire life to learn my Mage Gift, and you'll *work on it*?"

Russell shrugged. "I'm good at solving things, remember?"

I clenched my fists and exhaled heavily through my nose. After twenty-four years, I didn't know how patient I could be to not feel like a failure and a liar.

Russell stroked the stubble on his chin. "I *think* it only works with those who you don't actually know what their Mage Gift is. For example, you knew Calvin had the ability to apply makeup and make minor changes to facial extremities, but you had no way of knowing about the Gift given to him by the New Age God."

Russell furrowed his brows. "Ugh, maybe I'm wrong. If he's loaning Gifts through Melton gems, how were you able to see it in the vision?" He rubbed his face with his hands and suddenly looked haggard.

Russell's mind obviously was going off on another thought and topic. Something told me he wasn't talking to me anymore.

"Anyway," he said, shaking his head, "your Gift may prove quite useful in the future."

I threw the ring up a few inches and caught it in my hand. "How?"

"I want to use you."

I narrowed my eyes.

Russell shook his head and let out a short chuckle. "No, nothing terrible. But I think your

Mage Gift would prove quite an asset when solving crime. Your necklaces could even still be of good use. Especially..." Russell shifted his eyes downward and nervously twiddled his thumbs. "I want to catch the New Age God, Julie. No, I *will* catch him."

I didn't answer. I didn't know what to say.

Russell continued: "The best option is to keep your Gift secret. Even from your family. An ability like yours is enviable and could be used as a weapon. But we want it to be *our* weapon."

I held up my hands to stop him. "Russell, I—I'm not a police officer. *You're* not a police officer!"

"There is no law against people working independently to solve crimes and take on cases."

I chewed on my tongue as I thought. There was no denying the thrill I felt when helping Russell solve John's murder, but the fact remained that it was dangerous, and my anxiety had come to a peak on more than one occasion.

"I don't know—"

"You don't have to answer now," Russell interrupted, "but you have no idea the ways you and I can change lives if we work together."

He leaned forward so close I could smell the alcohol on his breath.

"Just think about it, alright?"

And then Russell left. I didn't watch him go. I merely stared at the walls of Father's study. The paper on the walls was a deep red—very similar to blood. I remembered my first sight of John's mangled body on the floor, his blood pooling underneath his head, and the scrawled letters reading what Russell had determined as "Not Eliza" —the message John had left before taking his last breath. I remembered the helpless, terrified feeling of knowing a murderer had been in my home. There were plenty of people out there who wanted to hurt others. And if I could somehow contribute to making even *one* person receive the justice they deserved, I wanted to do it.

"Russell!" I called out, running through the door he had left open. "Wait for me!"

EPILOGUE

Laura

LAURA SMITH HUGGED THE HOOD OF HER THICK COAT around her face as the cold wind of the late night stung her eyes. Trudging through the rain and the muddy soil of the Melton Manor gardens caused a fiery ache in her legs. Not too long ago, she could walk from the manor to the meeting place without any labored breathing. But now, in her thirties, Laura dreaded the exertion of walking to the secret, nighttime monthly meetings. Leaders of the New Age God's Disciples mandated furtiveness; cab drivers or passersby would compromise the group's secrecy.

Tonight, though, she did not mind the strenuous trek. This time *she* had an interview with the leaders. *She* would stand before the disciples and give one of the most important (if not the *most* important) reports the group had ever heard.

Laura looked back at the manor. She had been working for the Meltons for more than a decade, but she felt her time as a maid would soon come to an end.

Smiling, Laura lifted her black skirts and strode onward, pushing through the ache in her limbs with almost a skip in her step.

~

THREE QUICK KNOCKS, then a rapid succession of tapping a single fingernail against the dark wood of the door. That was the password for entering the underground meeting place. The disciples had many places to converse and worship in both Pirbis North and South, but this one... The large, looming door hidden near the city's sewer system led to a room purposed for only essential meetings.

The sound of a bar sliding away from the door made Laura's skin tingle. She was so close. She had dreamt and prayed for such a moment for five years —ever since her initiation as a disciple.

"Sister Laura!"

Laura beamed at her compatriot. Robert had introduced her to the religion at a time she needed it the most. She owed everything to him.

Laura took in the man's familiar, crooked smile and gangly arms. But one thing was newly different about him.

"Brother Robert!" she gasped. "You have no hair left."

He chuckled and ran a hand over his melon head. The stars and moon above them glinted off it like he had a mirror atop his head.

"I always knew I would regret entering my forties. And now I know it's because I was destined to go bald."

Laura bit her lip to hold in a laugh. If anyone heard them, the entire group would be arrested.

"Come, come, Sister." Robert waved her inside, feeling a sudden sense of urgency after hearing the distant sound of footsteps and accompanying chatter.

It was dark inside, save for the glint of a candle at the end of their long path. Laura had been to this particular meeting place only once—for her initiation. It had been dark then, too, and the only face Laura had seen among the disciples was Robert's.

"How did it go?" His eyes lit up with eagerness, but his voice remained a whisper. They weren't supposed to discuss the mission, but the work was too exciting.

"It went very smoothly," Laura said. "Although, at one point, they attached me to some truth gems, but I wasn't asked any questions I had to answer with a lie."

Robert nodded thoughtfully. They walked for a few more moments in silence before he spoke again.

"You remember what to do?"

Laura nodded, then remembering he couldn't see her, whispered a quick "Yes."

"Good. I'll be in the room. You just won't see me."

And with that, Robert left her side and took a quick turn. Laura hadn't even known there were multiple pathways in the hall.

She inhaled deeply, then quickly regretted it as the smell of rat feces and mold burned the insides of her nose. Her hard soles clicked loudly against the stone floor, piercing through the silence so starkly, she feared outsiders might be able to hear.

The soft glow of a single candle drew closer and closer until Laura stood directly in front of it. She clenched her fists to keep her excitement at bay, then slowly lifted her chin to the looming darkness before her.

"Sister Laura Smith. Here to report to the leaders of our New Age God's Disciples."

Her voice echoed many feet in front of her. There was no way to know how large the room was or how many people sat before her. The candle in front of her only provided enough light to illuminate the silhouette of the person reporting. The one other time she stood before it was for her initiation. She remembered it well: The booming voice asking her to repeat the oath promising faith in and dedication toward the New Age God and paving his way to take Othos' place as God for all of Dagirus.

"Sister." The voice was sweet, almost dripping like honey in Laura's ears as it reached her from the pitch dark. "You may begin."

"The first step of the New Age God's plan is complete," Laura projected with a proud smile. "The inspector has returned to the game, and I am positive our God is about to acquire what he needs from Calvin Sexton."

"Excellent," the disembodied voice said. "Then it is time to commence with Step Two."

NOTE FROM THE AUTHOR

Thank you for taking the time to read my book! It means the world to me. If you enjoyed it, it would be so helpful if you could leave a review on Amazon or Goodreads—

"I'm interrupting the author to say something important. Yes, this is Russell Gaines. And before you ask, no, I'm not an inspector—no matter what the title of this book says. But the author didn't want to call it 'Former Inspector Mage: Blood on the Floor.'

Anyway, be sure to leave a review. I need to find that bastard New Age God, and I can't do that unless the author is motivated to write more books. Much appreciated."

-Russell Gaines and Aleese Hughes

ACKNOWLEDGMENTS

Wow! It has been quite the journey. I came up with the *Inspector Mage* idea years ago. Granted, it did not start as much of an idea. All I knew was that I wanted to combine my two favorite book genres: fantasy and murder mystery. I wrote six other books before I even got to this story. I grew as a writer, I grew as a person, and then I felt ready to approach my biggest project yet.

I'm so grateful for this story. Russell and Julie have become a part of me, and I'm so excited to continue writing about them. So, of course, I want to thank them first. Russell and Julie are as real to me as this book in your hands. I also want to extend my deepest gratitude to my husband, Aaron, and my wonderful kids for their unparalleled love and support. And I can't go on without acknowledging the incredible feedback and assistance from my editors.

There are a few other people I am indebted to as well. Without them and their helpful contributions, I wouldn't have been able to publish this book. And here they are:

Andy Hughes
Jason Hughes
Mara Hughes
Marty Hughes
Stan Smith
Carol Thomas
Steve Vincent
Teresa Vincent
Linda Willingham

Again, I am grateful for all who were instrumental in the making of this book. Like my parents, my siblings, my cousin Aubrey, my cover designer Christine Horner, and so many others who have been there for me every step of the way.

But, of course, I can't finish an acknowledgment without thanking you! My readers! Authors are nothing without you guys. I love you all!

ABOUT THE AUTHOR

Aleese Hughes is many things: a mother and wife, an avid reader, a performer, and an author. Aleese enjoys her time at home with her children and relishes the opportunities to pick up a good book or write one herself.

Having grown up around theater her entire life, Aleese has a natural ability when it comes to charming audiences while on stage. And the same goes for her knack to put words to paper and create stories that people of all ages can read and enjoy.

The fantasy genre is not only her favorite to read, but it is also what she writes. As an up-and-coming

Young Adult Fantasy author, she's excited to share her stories with the world.

Learn more about Aleese Hughes and her books at aleesehughes.com or inspectormage.com.

facebook.com/aleesehugh

twitter.com/AleeseHughes

instagram.com/aleesehughes

Q & A

1. How do you get inspired to write?

This is a loaded question. I believe writing and creating stories has always been a noble thing to do. Can you imagine what our world would be like without these stories? I think it would be pretty dull. Since the beginning of time, people have found entertainment and solace in stories, whether it was a tale told by their grandfather at the campfire, an ancient Greek play, or a best-selling book.

I guess I've always felt a pull toward a writing career. There's something special about creating characters that can become real people to my readers. I like to make people *feel* something when they read--just how I want to make people feel something when

I'm on stage performing. The arts exist, in my opinion, to bring people the deep emotions they need to experience to relate with the rest of humanity.

I guess, to answer this question, I feel grateful to be one among the many to bring such joy to the world. If I can bring a single smile to someone's face, all the time I've spent writing is worth it.

2. How did you get the *Inspector Mage* idea?

I've always known I wanted to write a series that combined my two favorite genres: fantasy and murder mystery. It wasn't until I wrote six other books that had nothing to do with it before I felt ready to approach the concept. Russell was a whole other project in himself. I knew I wanted a talented and clever detective in my story. Russell is both of those things, but I was pleased to see his character change as I wrote the story. He can be harsh and arrogant, but he has a soft side he doesn't allow many people to see. I'm excited to share his character arc with you all in the following two books.

Julie is an anxious person. She is intelligent and adventurous, but social situations and shame take her over in ways that can become crippling. If I'm honest, I took a lot of my own feelings and experiences and applied them to Julie's character. I resonate with her on a deep level, and I know others out there do as well.

We'll see where the story goes! I have a pretty good idea of how it will end, but I won't divulge any of that.

3. What is the first book you ever read?

I picked up the first *Harry Potter* book when I was just five years old. I don't even remember learning how to read--my parents tell me I was quick and picked it with no issue. I tore through those *Harry Potter* books as they each came out. That series is what made me want to become an author. I wanted to make people feel the way J.K. Rowling made me feel with those stories.

4. What is your favorite book?

This is a tricky question. My favorite book would probably be one written by Brandon Sanderson. If I *had* to pick one of his books as my favorite, it would be *The Way of Kings*. That book is a masterpiece. There's no other word for it.

5. Will you be writing more after *The Inspector Mage Trilogy* is finished?

Yes, yes, a thousand times yes! I have so many ideas and outlines prepped and ready to go for more stories. I *never* want to stop writing!

ALSO BY ALEESE HUGHES

Inspector Mage: The Hanging Priest

WILL BE AVAILABLE IN 2022

The Tales and Princesses Series

BOOK ONE: PEAS AND PRINCESSES

BOOK TWO: APPLES AND PRINCESSES

BOOK THREE: PUMPKINS AND PRINCESSES

BOOK FOUR: BEASTS AND PRINCESSES

After the Tales and Princesses—A Set of Novellas

NOVELLA ONE: JANICE WALLANDER: A NOVELLA
RETELLING THE TALE OF RUMPELSTILTSKIN

NOVELLA TWO: QUEEN DALIA CHAR: A NOVELLA
RETELLING THE TALE OF ROSE RED